Louisa Morgan

Baron Bruno

Or, the unbelieving philosopher, and other fairy stories

Louisa Morgan

Baron Bruno
Or, the unbelieving philosopher, and other fairy stories

ISBN/EAN: 9783744750370

Printed in Europe, USA, Canada, Australia, Japan

Cover: Foto ©Andreas Hilbeck / pixelio.de

More available books at **www.hansebooks.com**

OR,

THE UNBELIEVING PHILOSOPHER,

And other Fairy Stories.

BY

LOUISA MORGAN.

WITH ILLUSTRATIONS BY R. CALDECOTT.

London:

MACMILLAN AND CO.

1875.

CONTENTS.

LIST OF ILLUSTRATIONS.

BARON BRUNO AND THE STARS;

OR,

The Unbelieving Philosopher.

BARON BRUNO AND THE STARS;

OR,

The Unbelieving Philosopher.

BARON BRUNO was the Prime Minister of the Hereditary Grand Duke of Rumpel Stiltzein. Besides being Prime Minister, he was the cleverest man in the kingdom. This is saying a good deal, for were there not (besides all the men of science, the physicians, the literati, and the great philosophers of the day) the General-in-Chief of the Grand-Ducal army, Prince Edlerkopf; the great High Almoner, Herr von Pfenig; and also the accomplished Graf von Wild Kranz, the most able lawyer and the politest man about court? So humble and gentle, indeed, were his manners, that strangers sometimes took it upon themselves to dispute the opinion of their modest neighbour. But such hardy persons seldom repeated the experiment after Wild Kranz had completely overturned their arguments in his quiet, hesitating tone, with a shrewd glance of enjoyment twinkling in his small wary eye; and woe to the man who a second time opposed his will or challenged his decision.

Very different was Baron Bruno. Impetuous, fiery, and caustic, gifted with inexhaustible memory, and brimming over with barbed sarcasm, he was often misunderstood and disliked in the outer world, but invariably beloved by those who knew him intimately.

Pfenig and Edlerkopf were devoted friends, as well as ministers at court. They had been educated together, and while Edlerkopf lent to the counsels of state the aid of wise and deliberate judgment and the weight of his nobly impartial character, Pfenig was the most wonderful manager of the public purse, and could not only calculate the incoming revenue within a hairsbreadth, but could also regulate government expenditure so exactly as to keep all departments amply supplied, and yet preserve a due regard to economy.

You may well imagine that with four ministers such as these the Grand Duke had little difficulty in maintaining peace and contentment in his beautiful kingdom of Rumpel Stiltzein; and that from every side artisans, labourers, and mechanics flocked to the small domain, within whose narrow boundaries prosperity sat enthroned. To add to his happiness, the Grand Duchess became the proud mother of twin children, the spirited handsome Prince Bertrand and the lovely gentle Princess Berta. They were now in their tenth year, and seemed only born to give pleasure and hope to their parents and to the whole principality.

Edlerkopf, Wild Kranz and Pfenig were all married, but Bruno had a solitary home ; and no one without ocular demonstration would have believed in what a shabby den this great statesman passed much of his time. In his town-house he had magnificent saloons, where all that was fair and choice delighted his guests ; but near the roof of this dwelling, and far above the haunts of men, there, like the eagle, Bruno had his eyrie, where, with ill-concealed impatience, he would hardly even permit the cleaning incursions of his maids, and few and far between were the footsteps that trod those time-worn boards. Here the Baron sat surrounded by dusty piles of books, now poring intently over the records of the past, now eagerly scanning the papers of the day, now striding up and down the narrow chamber, composing his speech for the Reichstag, or dashing off answers to his numerous correspondents. There also at the threshold would pause the faithful messengers who bore from minister to minister the secret boxes of state papers, and waited to obtain from each his signature before proceeding on their rounds.

A few steps and a small door led from the sanc-

tuary which I have described to the roof. Here
Bruno had a little observatory on one side fitted
up with a revolving cupola; so that when he sat in
the centre of this round miniature house he could
turn his telescope, without himself moving, upon any
part of the heavens, and seek with keen unfaltering eye the verification of calculations he had made,
or diligently mark the alteration and movement
among the visible planets. But the rest of the roof
was a free uncovered space, upon which a comfortable
chair and rug, generally kept within the observatory,
to be safe from the wear and tear of the elements,
were often placed. From this lonely elevated seat the
Baron would then study the myriads of stars with
his own unaided and unerring vision, until they
became to him dear and well-known companions.

During such silent hours of the night, when all
around teemed with nature's glorious presence, Bruno
indulged in long soliloquies. Sometimes he pondered
curiously over the strange difference between himself
and his colleagues. He well knew that, when weary
with the lengthened debates and vitiated air of the
Reichstag (which often extended its sittings till long
after midnight), Pfenig and Edlerkopf hastened home
to their faithful wives, and derived from their society
a pleasure little short of bliss; and found endless
interest in watching and fostering the mental and

physical growth of their children ; while Wild Kranz, though often delayed in his law chambers till near daybreak, (the keenest and hardest lawyer of his day,) considered no happiness like the sacred domestic felicity he also experienced when surrounded by his family. When these and other similar reflections weighed on Bruno's mind, he would lift his piercing eyes heavenward, and, shrugging his shoulders, murmur, half aloud : " O, ye stars ! ye are wife and children to me. As I gaze alone on you by night, I feel a secret satisfaction surpassing the keenest emotions experienced by these weak dreamers in their so-called felicity. O, immortal heavens ! enfold me in your vast space, and teach a finite mortal to comprehend in faint measure your infinite beauty and eternal unswerving laws." Bruno's fervid nature suffered no chill from such midnight exposure ; his iron frame was proof against fatigue ; his restless intellect but seldom needed or courted repose.

It was a hot night in July, worried and jaded, after a wearisome debate in the Reichstag, the Baron walked through the empty streets. The latest revellers were already housed, a strange hush hung over the noisy, populous city, and refreshing breezes blew on his burning brow, as he at length reached his home, and ascended to his upper chamber. With a sigh of contentment he stepped on the roof, and prepared to enjoy his well-earned repose. Throwing himself into his easy-chair, and drawing his soft rug across his feet, he became absorbed in the contemplation of the firmament above.

As the night wore on, thoughts, till now strangers to him, took possession of his mind. A new yearning for companionship awoke in his world-wearied bosom. In vague, uneasy discontent with his solitary condition, he turned restlessly from side to side, and at length exclaimed aloud : " To you, distant stars ! I nightly offer the homage of a constant worshipper ; would that you in return could give me to know the spell of love, and teach me what it is that inspires the painter, the`poet, and the lover."

Hardly had the thought crossed his mind, or the half-uttered words risen to his lips, when a meteor fell swiftly rushing from the stars on which he gazed. He strove to follow it with his eye, but was dazzled by the blinding flash of light. For a moment fire seemed to surround him. When the bright glow became less intense, lo ! upon the roof near at hand, where that vivid ray had fallen, shone a shimmering shape. The dreamer started from his chair. Bewildered and entranced, he deemed her the creature of his imagination ; and surely mortal eye had never beheld a form so fair. In trailing garments of palest azure there stood the perfect ideal of a poet's dream.

THE DREAMER STARTED FROM HIS CHAIR.   P. 5.

From her hair gleamed a faint effulgence, and her deep tender eyes sent a strange thrill to the philosopher's heart.

The burden of many years fell from Bruno; the ardour of youth rushed through his veins; ambition, politics, calculations, all disappeared like fallen leaves before the autumn wind; and in agitated tones he besought his beautiful visitant to tell him whence she came.

" Son of earth! " replied the fair unknown, "thou hast watched and loved our stars for long years. We in our turn have known thee, and have guarded thee and thy fortunes in many a time of danger. Thou wouldest know the spell of love. It is even now awakening within thy rugged breast; but beware! Thou hast disbelieved in immortality, and doubted the eternal power of our great Creator. We love thee! we yearn to save thy soul! We long to soften thee through human affection; that when thy poor earth is no more, thou mayst find an everlasting home, where

> ' Infinite day excludes the night,
> And pleasures banish pain.'   ·

I—Alcyone, sent by my sisters—I am here to speed thine upward way."

Bruno, spell-bound, eagerly listened. Deeply ena-

moured of the lovely messenger, he succeeded in win-
ning from the fair denizen of the stars her consent to
remain with him on one condition. She stipulated
that she should be permitted every month to spend
the evening hours of this self-same night entirely
alone beneath the canopy of heaven, without interruption or intrusion, for her life depended on the due
observance of this time of "retreat."

She also added, falteringly, that if her faith were
once doubted she must quit for ever the pleasant
paths of human fellowship, and be claimed again by
her immortal sisters. The Baron gladly vowed to
keep what seemed to him such wondrously simple
promises by which to gain so peerless a bride. The
time passed swiftly as these arrangements were made,
and ere long the first streaks of daylight appeared in
the east. Alcyone, faint and weary, was conducted
to a chamber for rest and repose ; and the Baron
aroused his servants and informed them that he was
about to be married.

In the country of Rumpel Stiltzein it was customary
to celebrate marriages in the evening; there were
therefore still available a good many hours for the
requisite preparations.

The court of the Grand Duke was considerably
agitated by the unexpected news. Strange rumours
were set afloat regarding the newly-elected bride. The

Prime Minister's answer to all inquiries was the same. He let it be understood that the Lady Alcyone was an orphan relative lately committed to his charge; that she had suddenly arrived from the country the evening before, when he came to the conclusion that the best way of taking care of her would be to marry her, and having gained the lady's consent, all was well.

It is true that Bruno had a private interview with his Prince; but as it was held with closed doors, the substance of their conversation is unknown. The only thing certain is, that the Grand Duke himself consented to give away the bride.

Edlerkopf, Pfenig and Wild Kranz, with their wives and families, and all the chief members of the court promised to attend at the ceremony, and great were the rejoicings that the solitary philosopher was about to enjoy the sweet pleasures of home life. All rejoiced, because they believed the change would be for the Baron's happiness; but there was one dissentient mind. The Countess Olga von Dunkelherz, one of the ladies-in-waiting on the Grand Duchess, was a spinster of a certain age, and of undisputed ability; celebrated for her witty tongue and smart sayings. She was not displeased when rumour coupled her name with that of the Prime Minister, and when the courtiers rallied her about the Baron's attentions. The truth was that Bruno had never for

a moment regarded her in the light of his future
Baroness; her manners wanted the repose and softness which to him constituted a woman's chief charm.
In spite of her masterly intellect, her conversation
often bored him. For in his moments of relaxation
he turned to the fair and softer sex for sympathy
and recreation, not to involve his wearied brain in
arguments about the last geological discovery, or
the newest theory of electricity.

But as he remained single, and they were constantly
together, the Countess Olga had insensibly grown to
regard him as her own property. Imagine therefore her astonishment and her displeasure when the
Grand Duchess, summoning her ladies to her apartment, gave them instructions to lay out her state
robes, and prepare for a grand court ceremonial, as
Baron Bruno's wedding was to take place that very
evening within the palace.

All was bustle and confusion; but the labours of
the court cook were something superhuman. It required, indeed, the utmost efforts of genius and in-
dustry combined to produce so splendid a feast at
such short notice. It is only due, however, to
Francabelli's reputation as first *chef* of the Grand
Duchy, if not of the world at large, to record that the
execution of his designs was on this occasion carried
out with peculiar success.

At last the nuptial hour approached, and excited curiosity was gratified by the sight of the bride, as she was led slowly through the palace by the Grand Duke. Her wondrous beauty amazed every one, as also the radiant simplicity of her attire. She wore her robes of flowing azure, and over her forehead there sparkled a gem of extraordinary brilliancy, which seemed absolutely to blaze with light.

As Alcyone advanced towards the altar, Baron Bruno, clad in his splendid court uniform, embroidered with gold, and covered with decorations, stepped forth to meet her, and the wedding ceremony was soon completed. The priest dipped his hand in the holy water and sprinkled some over bride and groom during his final benediction ; as he did so, the Countess Olga, who stood near with her royal mistress, rushed forward, exclaiming, " She is a witch ! she is a witch ! the holy water has scared her !" All eyes turned instantly on Alcyone, who shuddered visibly, and would have fallen to the ground where she knelt had not her husband's strong arm encircled and held her up. A mortal pallor overspread her fair countenance, and, strange to relate, the glittering gem on her forehead became opaque, and was clouded over with a dim moisture. By the aid of strong perfumes she gradually revived, but was thoroughly shaken and

overcome. Baron Bruno, therefore, craving the indulgence of the Grand Duke, begged permission to
retire at once with his bride, and entreated that their
absence should not be allowed to cast a shadow over
the rejoicings at court.

Now Bombastes, the Grand Duke, though of a
choleric temperament, was still at heart a man of
just and keen perception. He perceived that the
newly-made baroness was indisputably over-fatigued,
and that it was only natural her bridegroom should
wish to take every care of her. He instantly,
therefore, granted his Prime Minister's request, and
calling the other great officers of state around him,
invoked their aid to carry on the court revels with
due spirit and merriment ; at the same time adding,
in an undertone, that he trusted his faithful servant
had not undone himself by marrying an unknown
beauty without parents, relations, or antecedents !

The three ministers, Edlerkopf, Pfenig, and Wild
Kranz, with their wives and children, joined heart
and soul in the gaieties of the evening. The children, with their friends Prince Bertrand and Princess Berta, were, as a great treat, allowed to
sit up to supper, and had a small side-table to
themselves. Here old Donnerfuss, the head butler,
kept them well supplied with all they demanded,
and they behaved with decorum for a considerable

time. At length, wearied with the protracted courses, and finding it impossible to eat any more, the thoughtless boys amused themselves by sticking burrs on the footmen's silken calves as they passed to and fro. These naughty children had purposely provided themselves with a quantity of these instruments of torture, in hopes of finding some use for them during the dull state supper. For some time they pursued their fun unnoticed during the general bustle, and quite undisturbed by the muttered maledictions of their victims. At last Bombastes, having an observant eye, became aware of some interruption in the serving of the dinner. Looking round the hall, he noticed on every side agitated footmen carefully examining their lower extremities. In a voice of thunder he demanded of the Lord Chamberlain an explanation of such unprecedented behaviour. The Lord Chamberlain called up the High Steward of the Household, who, in his turn, required Donnerfuss to explain this breach of discipline. Thereupon the fifty red-faced footmen, seeing all eyes turned upon them, at once resumed their duties, regardless of pricking sensations about the leg and unseemly excrescences upon the otherwise fair white proportions of their well-filled stockings. Donnerfuss, in a frightened whisper, revealed the truth to the High Steward, and he, in his turn, narrated the mischievous

exploit of the boys to the Lord High Chamberlain. Bombastes now impatiently beckoned the latter
to his Grand-ducal chair, and insisted upon hearing
the whole root of the matter. Sanftschriften, who
was himself a parent, and naturally kind-hearted,
tried to soften down the affair; but as Bombastes
listened, his large, round, prominent eyes seemed as
if they would absolutely start from his head at the
recital of this outrage on decorum. He sternly commanded the culprits to retire to bed ; and, glancing
wrathfully at Edlerkopf, Pfenig, and Wild Kranz (who
sat quaking in their shoes), he added further : "As
to the well-brought-up sons of these great noblemen,
their domestic life is beyond the control of their poor
sovereign ; but for the next month I give orders
that no dessert of any kind shall pass the lips of
Prince Bertrand, who has thus misbehaved himself
in so shameful and public a manner." Princess
Berta and the other little girls, distressed at the
disgrace of their playmates, rose also at once from
the table, and accompanied them from the hall.
Thus it came to pass that the court children had
no very pleasant associations with the day of Baron
Bruno's wedding. Indeed, you may be very certain
that the three ministers gave their sons the same
punishment as Prince Bertrand ; and therefore for
a whole month the boys had good reason to re-

member the marriage feast, as their tutors, governesses, and nurses, were strictly enjoined to carry out the Grand Duke's peremptory edict. Princess Berta and the other small girls, tender and soft-hearted as little maidens ever should be, did their best to alleviate the punishment of their playmates by voluntarily depriving themselves of all sweet things for the same period, which, I am sure you will agree with me, required much self-denial, on the part of those dessert-loving damsels, and was no small proof of affection.

In the meantime Bruno had taken his bride to a small cottage he owned on the borders of a wide and gloomy forest. Here they passed the few days which, by the indulgence of his royal master, Bruno was enabled to spare from the affairs of state. When they were alone together, his wife expressed to him her conviction that some ill-disposed person had tampered with the holy water, so as to affect that which was sprinkled over them. She had also felt during the ceremony the near presence of an antipathetic and malign influence. Alcyone furthermore explained to her husband that the gem on her forehead was a talisman, which paled and grew dim on the approach of danger, or when exposed to poison. The Baron at once remembered the dull appearance presented by the jewel when the holy

C

water fell near it, but he also became unreasonably
vexed when his bride refused to loosen it, even for
one moment, from her hair, to permit him to examine
it in his hand.

He gradually grew to regard its brilliance with
a certain amount of suspicion, and more than once,
when the gentle Alcyone laid her head upon his
shoulder, he felt as if a fiery eye shone guardian
over her and watched unsleepingly his every movement. When in his vexation Bruno allowed himself
to speak harshly for the first time to his young wife,
Alcyone tearfully deprecated his displeasure. She
assured him her life was bound up in her talisman,
and that if she parted with it, for ever so brief a
space, she must at once return to the regions whence
she came. After this explanation Bruno rarely referred to the disputed point, but it is not too much
to say that the lurid ray of the strange gem often
in their happiest moments sent a sudden thrill to
his heart's core, and gave a feeling of insecurity to
his most private hours of retirement.

> " It is the little rift within the lute
> That by and by will make the music mute,
> And, ever widening, slowly silence all.
>
> " The little rift within the lover's lute,
> Or little pitted speck in garnered fruit,
> That rotting inwards slowly moulders all."

I have already hinted that Bruno was of a sceptical turn of mind. Possessed of rare intellectual powers, he had studied metaphysics to such an extent, and become so thoroughly master of the strange theories propounded by the deep-thinking German philosophers of the day, that he could not bend himself to the simplicity of that religion which only demands the faith of a little child; he disbelieved the immortality of the soul, and professed to doubt the existence of a future state.

But though he and his bride widely differed in faith, yet day by day she became more and more endeared to him, by the lovely nature of her mind no less than by the graces of her person. Her exceeding humility and true-hearted simplicity showed to him in a new light those religious duties at which in less peaceful days he was wont to cavil. Well would it have been for both could their lives have been thus spent far from the busy world, in the calm retreat, where for the first time the gray-haired man recalled soft prayers which a mother's lips (long since silent and cold) had murmured over his infant head.

But the calls of duty had to be obeyed, and ere long the prime minister and his bride returned to Aronsberg, to take their place at court and in society, and to have endless fêtes and receptions given in their honour. Here Alcyone's gentle unassuming

manners, added to her great beauty, made her
a universal favourite. The malicious Gräfin von
Dunkelherz, however, disseminated strange stories
concerning the new Baroness, and aroused the suspicions of those who were already perhaps somewhat
jealous of the many charms united in the fair person
of the young stranger.

Amid the series of festivities given in honour of the
newly-married couple, it was observed that whenever a
storm of thunder and lightning broke over the neighbourhood Alcyone was painfully agitated. Wherever
she and her husband might be, she implored him
to convey her home as soon as possible; the electric
influence so entirely overcame her that more than
once she seemed completely gone—so utterly did she
lose colour and consciousness—so deadly pale did she
become. To Bruno's impetuous nature this unfortunate tendency proved a serious annoyance. He
considered that by a little firm exercise of moral
courage his wife could have retained her senses.
Often after conveying her home and reappearing
alone (by her earnest request) at some state banquet,
he would be universally rallied about her captious-
ness, and even made to see (owing to Olga's kind
offices) that his friends considered the whole affair in
a somewhat mysterious light. It will be remembered
that Alcyone stipulated for one night of retirement

every month, when, undisturbed and alone, she spent
long solitary hours upon the roof. She entreated
Bruno, by all his affection for her, neither to approach
the place himself nor to suffer any one else to intrude
upon her privacy. Somehow or other this circum-
stance, with numerous additions, became bruited
abroad, and it was whispered that the Baron's wife
was in regular communication with demons. Bribed
and listening servants heard voices of no earthly
timbre, speaking in an unknown language. More they
were unable to say, for Bruno as yet kept faithful
guard over his wife's hours of mystic retreat.

At last, however, the time approached when the
sittings of the Reichstag terminated, and when
all who could forsook the dusty purlieus of the
town for the mountains, the sea, or their country
dwellings. People began to be too busy making their
own plans to attend to those of their neighbours,
and Bruno retired once more with his Baroness to
Tiefträume Forest. There in their small cottage, with
its low long veranda covered with creepers, they
spent weeks—nay, months—of uninterrupted happiness. On one side of their home patches of wild
moorland were beautifully interspersed with cultivated
oases of garden. Towards the east rose the dark
masses of the pine forest, giving with their sombre
colouring an ever-fresh beauty to the foreground of

lovely flowering shrubs. Passing through tangled masses of bramble and fern, the path led by bare gray rocks and tufts of purple heather to some ivy-covered bower ; or you came upon some exquisite smooth-shaven little lawn, jewelled in bright patterns of many coloured flowers, and adding brilliance and perfume to the scene.

Here Alcyone and her husband wandered toge-ther, or, perhaps descending the steps at the end of their garden, stood on the brink of the little river Naecken, which tumbled and hurried through its nar-row rocky channel, thus dividing them from the forest. Lower down the streamlet formed a small lake, on which a boat was kept, and where Bruno was wont to row his wife, and try to teach her unskilful hand to guide the oar. He laid these lines beside her one morning towards the end of their country sojourn when, fresh and fair as Aurora herself, she took her place at their morning meal :—

> " One moment let me live the time again,
>   The sweet, sweet time when o'er the silvery loch
>   The frail bark sped, or hand-in-hand we climbed
>   Together, where the divided mountain path
>   Stopped like a thing perplexed, or haply stood
>   To watch yon dark blue vault where white clouds sailed
>   Onward and onward through the homeless sky ;
>   Or when, returning from a mid-day ride,
>   We turned to gaze where far-off heathery vales
>   Gleamed between shadowy hills, and dark woods rained

BARON BRUNO AND ALCYONE. P 22.

Transparent sunshine through their golden leaves.
And sweet it was to rob the miser night,
Of her rich hours, as side by side we sat,
Seeking to chain the time that fled too fast,
By mazy labyrinths of sweet discourse ;
These things can never die—there is no death
Of happy feelings, gentlest sympathies,
And that delicious sadness, whose deep tints
Fall like soft shadows o'er the sunny past.
Therefore in years to come a calm, clear voice,
Like a stray note of some forgotten tune,
Shall rise from out these happy autumn days,
Waking a melody of gentler thoughts
Through all the silent chambers of my heart."

The Baron was often obliged to return to town for a day on important business, or to attend his royal master at the Prince's Château ; but Alcyone never wearied when alone with nature; and these little separations lent a new delight to the hour of reunion. Jaded and tired from his hot journey, Bruno would then seat himself in the veranda and recount to his fondly-listening wife all the little adventures of the day, while her cool, soft hand laid on his burning brow, or her gentle voice, carolling forth low songs in the silent twilight, soothed and refreshed his hard-worked brain. It was at times like these, when husband and wife were drawn very near, that Alcyone spoke of her faith, and allowed him to see and know the firm unfaltering trust that possessed her simple mind. She sometimes referred to the possibility of their separation—to her hope of ultimate reunion. When, however, she had but half uttered such words, Bruno, enfolding her in his arms, with a quivering voice would beseech her to be silent, and not break his heart.

Autumn disappeared, and next came winter with all its delightful accompaniments of snow and sleighing. Merrily tinkled the bells and fast flew the steeds under Bruno's skilful guidance, as their gaily-decorated sledge was whirled through the broad thoroughfares and snowy parks of Aronsberg. Christmas also passed by, and Santa Klaus sent joy to the hearts of myriads of children with his mysterious gifts. Months again rolled away, and the glad Easter Feast was in full celebration when, with the first sweet violets, came a dear little child to bless and brighten the home of Alcyone and her husband. They called her Violet because she bloomed into life at the same time as those fragrant flowers, and Stella was added in remembrance of the sacred mystery known only to her parents. In the fulness of his joy, Bruno dismissed, as he thought for ever, from his mind the cruel unworthy thoughts he had once been led to entertain of his bride. It would be difficult to describe this infant to those who never saw her; but let each one think of all the children he has been privileged to know. If among such dear ones he can recall some babe of a beauty too rare and fair to attain to maturity in this bleak world, then he may in some faint degree picture to himself the nameless charm that surrounded the little Violet as with a halo.

Various changes now for a time partially relieved the Baron from official duties; wrapped up in his domestic happiness, nearly a year passed swiftly by before he was once more drawn into the unceasing whirl of political and social court life.

It was already June, the busiest season in the Aronsberg world. Plunged in the necessary rounds of visiting and receiving, the Baroness had but little time to enjoy, as she wished, the society either of her husband or of the little Violet, now at a most engaging age. It is true that it was totally against her own wish that Alcyone took so active a part in the gay world. Bruno, whom nature had formed to shine in society, and gifted with marvellous conversational powers, chafed under her continual excuses, and, returning with eager zest to his old life, insisted upon the Baroness assuming that prominent place in society which was hers by right as the wife of the Prime Minister.

It was about this time that the artful Countess Olga began once more to drop poisoned words about the court concerning Alcyone. Ever on the alert to open the Baron's eyes to the folly of what she called his strange infatuation, she eagerly hailed the first signs of

coolness between him and his wife. In an unguarded
moment Bruno let fall some hasty expression regarding her absence from a court ball, and Olga, with
honeyed words, sympathizing in his disappointment,
hinted that rumour credited the Baroness with some
private amusement at home, she so rarely vouchsafed to favour the court with her presence for more
than the briefest possible attendance at the levees of
the Grand Duchess.

Bruno's conscience smote him while he listened to
the Countess von Dunkelherz's ill-natured remarks.
He answered somewhat shortly that the little Violet
being an only child and very delicate, absorbed
much of her mother's attention, and therefore she
had the best of excuses for remaining at home. A
beginning had nevertheless been made, and Olga
took good care to keep up her renewed intimacy
with the Prime Minister.

It may have been the vitiated town air which
now affected Violet's health; but she sensibly
drooped, and caused her mother the keenest anxiety.
Her father (prompted by his evil adviser,) although
affectionate and kind, deemed his wife fanciful when
she fretted over the child's altered appearance, and
became more and more displeased if Alcyone
absented herself from society.

There was to be a grand masked ball in honour of

Prince Bertrand and Princess Berta's birthday. They were allowed to choose their own diversion, and they fixed that their father and the Grand Duchess should appear as Oberon and Titania, and that every guest should personate some fairy character. All was excitement, while the Grand Duke himself, assisted by the court painter, and somewhat guided by the predilections of his children, chose the dress to be worn by each visitor, and had it written on the card of invitation. Berta and her brother settled to represent Prince Hempseed and his sister Olivia. Other heroes and heroines too numerous to be recorded were selected. Snow-white and Rose-red, the Blue Bird, the Yellow Dwarf, Beauty and the Beast, Cinderella, and many others found suitable representatives, but the Prime Minister and his wife were requested to become, for the time being, Puss in Boots and the White Cat. At one o'clock all masks were to be removed, and a complete transformation-scene enacted, as regarded many of the characters, who would at that hour, like the White Cat and Cinderella, throw off their disguise, and, uncovering their faces, shine forth resplendent in garments the most exquisite that could be devised for the occasion. Then, marshalled in due rank, the King and Queen of Fairyland proposed to lead their motley subjects to supper. The fun grew fast and furious in the little

court of Rumpel Stiltzein. Desperate were the
efforts of the tailors, milliners, and shoemakers to
meet the multifarious demands made on their time,
which was very short; and on their invention, which
was taxed to the utmost.

Alcyone from the first disliked the idea of the
ball, and all the rampant merriment connected with
it. Her ailing child required constant care, and she
herself felt far from strong. She mooted the question
of remaining at home, but Bruno would not hear of this,
and indeed answered her so reproachfully when she
proposed it, that she made up her mind to sacrifice
her own desires, and please him by endeavouring to
throw herself heartily into the affair. During the
many necessary discussions with the other court
ladies as to the all-important subject of dress, the
Baroness was left alone with Olga, who of late had,
to all appearance, been her most sympathizing friend.
The crafty Countess soon extracted from Alcyone the
little history of her own reluctance to appear, her
husband's consequent displeasure, and her determination to gratify him by paying every possible attention
to her dress.

The eventful evening at length arrived. Baron
Bruno, after an early dinner, was compelled to attend
for a short period an important sitting of the Reichstag. His house was at some distance from the public

offices of state ; he therefore took his fancy ball-dress with him, and settled to change his attire in his own small official room, while Alcyone should start at a later hour, and call for him on her way to the palace. Alcyone felt unusually sad as her husband waved her a hasty adieu and speeded off to the Reichstag. He strictly enjoined her to observe due punctuality in her engagements, as the Grand Duke wished to enter the ballroom in a grand procession formed of all his chief ministers and officers of state, court ladies, and hereditary noblemen.

Violet had perceptibly drooped more and more, though her fond father refused to see the change. He only, however, saw his little daughter at brief intervals of his busy. life, when a flush of delight at his approach rounded her pale cheeks, and her dark-blue eyes sparkled with the keen joy of being tossed or fondled in his arms.

After Bruno's departure, Alcyone ascended the nursery stairs, and found Violet already in bed, but restless and uneasy, and tossing to and fro. The large windows stood wide open, though very little air seemed as yet to stir among the trees of the square in which they lived.

The mother sat down beside her child. The baby was at once comforted, and held out its little arms to be taken to her bosom. Alcyone lifted her from the cot, and, dismissing the maids, seated herself by the window in a low rocking-chair, and crooned soft lullabies to her infant. The babe did not yet sleep, but she lay soothed and quiet, gazing into her mother's sweet face, and smiling when she caught the bright sparkling of the radiant gem.

Suddenly the peaceful scene was changed; with a troubled cry the little Violet started up, and at the same instant Lady Olga stood in the doorway. Hardly apologising for her unexpected appearance in the Baroness's private apartments, Olga unfolded her extraordinary plan. After expressing great sympathy for the child's indisposition, and professing to understand fully Alcyone's distressing position, she asked leave to proceed at once to the Baroness's dressing-room, and there and then array herself in the garments of the "White Cat." As she and Alcyone were much the same height and size, this change of dress could be very easily accomplished, and would form an indistinguishable disguise; she then further proposed to set off in the carriage and personate the fair young Baroness at the ball. At first Alcyone would not listen to her artful suggestion, justly fearing the displeasure of her husband; but Olga assured her that long before the deception must at any rate cease (on the unmasking at one o'clock) she would, using the privilege of an old acquaintance, explain the whole affair to Baron Bruno, and represent to him aright the mother's fears for her child. Indeed those fears seemed but too well founded, for since Olga's entrance the baby had grown wild and feverish, and kept up an incessant moaning as if in actual pain. Harassed and perplexed therefore, Alcyone at length yielded a reluctant consent, and, ringing the bell, ordered lights to be placed in her dressing-room, and attendance to be given to aid the Countess von Dunkelherz in her somewhat difficult toilet. One consideration which weighed much with Alcyone in her final decision, was the unfortunate coincidence that this happened to be the very night of her monthly retirement — that mysterious proceeding of which her husband had now grown so impatient that she was fain never to mention it, but strove to accomplish her purpose as best she might without attracting his attention. She had all the time hoped to slip away unnoticed from the ball, but she well knew this would be a very difficult matter to accomplish, as besides her own timidity about leaving the palace by herself, her extreme beauty made her remarkable in whatever society she moved.

Still it was with a foreboding of evil she resolved for the first time to act without her husband's knowledge, and remain unbidden at home.

It is scarcely necessary to add that Olga, from frequent inquiries and a diligent system of espionage, was well aware of the mysterious and so-called solitary hours entered upon by the Baroness at stated intervals, and she was equally cognisant of the fact that the wonted period had arrived for the observance of this strange custom, and had laid her plans accordingly.

The evening wore on ; after the noisy departure of the carriage containing its unusual occupant, all within the house became peaceful and silent. Without was heard the ceaseless hum of the busy city, but faint, far, and mellowed by distance. Overhead the stars twinkled cheerfully forth from the blue bed on which they had lain fast asleep during the hot reign of the sun.

> It is twilight in the city,
>   And the sun has sunk afar,
> Where a brightness gilds the pathway
>   Of the quiet evening star.
>
> Dimly in the hazy distance
>   Twinkle all the myriad eyes
> Glittering far into the darkness,
>   Where the mighty city lies.
>
> Twittering through the leafy branches,
>   Birds are calling soft and low,
> Scarcely heard amid the humming
>   Of the city's ceaseless flow.

Yet I hear their gentle voices,
 And their evening hymn of love,
While the stars are clearer shining,
 From the dark-blue heaven above.

Happy children ! careless playing,
 In and out beneath the trees,
With your childish hair all streaming,
 Floating on the evening breeze.

Pure and blissful hours of childhood,
 Never prized until gone by,
Stay, oh ! stay a while ! and o'er me,
 Let your lingering radiance lie.

Leave a gleam of that bright sunshine
 Which was ours in days of yore,
Ere we parted for life's battle,
 Ere we left home's peaceful shore.

Voices then with ours were mingling,
 That on earth are silent now,
Arms around us fondly twining,
 That have long been still and low.

Yes—in gazing on the starlight,
 Fancy sometimes strives to trace
Forms beloved amid the twilight,
 Or a well-remembered face.

Angels now ! yet be our guardians,
 In this tearful vale below,
Shedding light around our pathway,
 Giving comfort as we go.

So when life's frail chord is loos'ning,
 And our eyes to sorrow close,
When the glorious morn is dawning
 O'er the long sad night of woes,

D

> Linger near us—that, when rising,
> We may—child-like—meet again
> Where the severed are united,
> Where the weary have no pain.

Ever and anon the deep musical bell of the Reichstag clock boomed forth amid the darkening shadows, telling of time's rapid progress and remorseless flight, yet giving to many of the dwellers in Aronsberg a feeling of joyful security and safety. For the tall tower stood over and among them like some mighty guardian whose ceaseless care and unsleeping vigilance kept watch amid the city by day and by night and with cheerful voice proclaimed his vicinity—thus oftentime becoming a loved companion to weary mortals whom sickness, separation, anxiety, or sorrow kept awake through the livelong night.

> Chime, Aronsberg bells, chime ceaselessly on,
> Till partings be over and weary work done.
> Boom o'er the broad waters, thou musical tone,
> Remorseless thy knell, and I sorrow alone,
> For perchance in my bosom shall waken no more,
> The rapture that thrilled to thy chiming of yore.

The baby now sank to rest in its tiny cot, a heavenly smile irradiated its little countenance, as if in some happy dream it was more than compensated for the uneasy hours of pain and unrest so lately experienced.

The hour of Alcyone's isolation approached:

wrapped in her long flowing robes, with her beautiful hair streaming over her shoulders, she bent over the sleeping Violet and dropt a kiss and murmured a blessing over her child ; then slowly ascended the narrow stair which led to Bruno's solitary chamber. The small door opened, then closed again with a spring, and all was still, while the nurses below, whispering together, knew their mistress was alone with the stars.

Nearly an hour passed by, and tranquillity reigned around ; most of the servants had gone to bed, those who remained up were in the lower and more distant parts of the house. Hasty sounds suddenly broke upon the still night air ; the Baron's champing steeds drew up in the courtyard ; Bruno himself, flushed and agitated, sprang rapidly up-stairs, followed by the ruthless Olga ! He pushed past his astonished domestics, noisily calling and seeking Alcyone in every room, including the nursery, where he roused and startled his sleeping child. Finally he ascended his own narrow stair, and entered the study. He paused at the small door so often described, and tapping, called his wife's name once or twice ; no response came ; without a moment's compunction, in excited passion, he drew the key from an inner pocket, and, unlocking the door he had solemnly promised to regard as sacred, threw it violently open.

D 2

With a loud grating noise the ill-fated portal swung back on its hinges, and disclosed to his bewildered eyes a wondrous sight. Around his wife stood five or six maidens of surpassing beauty; like her—yet unlike—for oh! how clearly he could see the marks of human sorrow and care which cast their shadow over her countenance alone. Each bore on her forehead a brilliant jewel resembling Alcyone's ; the most delicious perfume was wafted on the air, and an indescribable mellow glow of light emanated from and yet illuminated the lovely strangers. More than this he had not time to observe ; a terrible explosion shook the house to its foundation, and he became enveloped in a choking impenetrable vapour. Olga also, who, unobserved, with a bevy of terrified servants, had followed in his footsteps, was half suffocated, seeing, however, nothing of those radiant forms.

As the light breeze dissipated the stifling fumes, Alcyone, with sorrow and dismay imprinted on her gentle features, stood inquiringly before her husband, as if to demand some explanation of this sudden violation of their compact. But now a youth, whom Bruno had never before seen, stepped from behind Alcyone, with cold and majestic mien. Bowing gravely to the Baron, he thus addressed him, in low thrilling tones : " Behold in me, Hyas, the brother of Alcyone, come hither to aid and defend my sister in the hour of need. I demand a full examination into her conduct. Before others you have doubted her and intruded on her privacy—before others her character must be cleared!"

Stunned and bewildered by these swiftly succeeding events, Bruno's ready tongue for once completely failed him. Now—alas!—when too late, he bitterly regretted his precipitation, and the credence he had too easily lent to wicked and baseless insinuations.

Instead of keeping her promise to Alcyone, and explaining aright to the Baron his wife's unpremeditated absence, Olga had made out that the whole affair was a preconceived plot which she had been induced to conceal till the last moment. She had furthermore hinted that the gravest suspicions were aroused by the Baroness's non-appearance, which of course became universally known and commented upon at the hour of unmasking. At last she had so worked upon Bruno's ardent temperament that, forgetting everything save the jealousy of the moment, he rushed wildly home, causing quite a sensation at court and doing irreparable mischief to his domestic happiness.

In spite of his sister's tearful remonstrances, Alcyone's brother now demanded of the Baron when a public inquiry could be instituted; and on hearing ·that it was possible on the morrow, he instantly cited the affrighted Gräfin von Dunkelherz to appear and proffer her charge against the fair Alcyone, who for the first time recognised in the Countess a deadly enemy.

Hyas furthermore insisted on keeping watch over his sister and her child until Alcyone was proved beyond blame in the eyes of the world. They were left alone together. The baffled Olga slunk away to her home. Bruno, distressed and repentant, unavailingly paced his lonely chamber until morning arrived.

At the earliest possible moment (after the late carousals of the night before) the Prime Minister demanded an audience of his sovereign, and the matter being then fully explained, the Grand Duke commanded that the trial of the Baroness should take place at noon, in the Hochplatz, a large open space surrounded by public buildings and gardens, and not far from the Grand Ducal Palace. Bombastes, at Hyas' request, also sent criers in every direction to summon the people to attend, and by twelve o'clock the vast square was filled to overflowing.

The Grand Duke and Duchess, with the lords and ladies in waiting and other state officials, sat upon a raised platform in the centre, surrounded by a guard of honour. Edlerkopf, at the head of a brilliant staff of officers, kept the immense assembly from encroaching on the crimson daïs where accused and accuser were placed near at hand. Bruno, pale and heart-stricken, stood there. At some little distance Hyas and his sister sat together, their striking resemblance and singular beauty attracting every eye. It was observed that Hyas bore on his uncovered head a jewel almost surpassing in radiance that which sparkled on his sister's brow. Alcyone never raised her head, but bent over her child, whom she carried in her arms.

A profound silence reigned over the excited throng as Hyas bending low to the Duke, declared that his sister's honour had been tarnished by the foul aspersions cast upon it, and that he had traced many of these reports to the Countess von Dunkelherz; he therefore demanded that she should frankly say of what she accused the Baroness Bruno.

Olga, who by this time had entirely recovered from her previous confusion, now advanced. Craning her long neck, and glancing spitefully at the drooping form of the suffering Alcyone, she thus answered Hyas' summons :

"I charge the Lady Alcyone with being a witch. She cannot part, even for one moment, with the gem she bears on her forehead; she keeps mysterious assignations with beings from another world; and she

has so bewitched her husband, the acute and learned
Baron Bruno, that he is hardly accountable for his
actions."

At these cruel words an ominous murmur ran
through the crowd, and half stifled cries arose.—
"Burn the witch!"   "Deliver our Baron from her
spells!"   "Cut off root and branch—mother and
child!"   Such were some of the menaces hoarsely
muttered by the surging and fickle multitude.   It
was with no small difficulty that Edlerkopf, at the
head of his guards, restrained the populace from laying violent hands on the Baroness and her brother.
Hyas, cool and collected, waited until the gathering
tumult was in some measure quieted; his clear voice
then penetrated far and wide.   "Ye have heard, O
people," he exclaimed, "the voice of the traducer; ye
shall now give ear to unwilling testimony in favour
of the accused."

So saying he divested himself of his long-flowing
outer garment, and warning all around to preserve
strict silence, he drew a large circle round himself
and his sister, and also compelled the Countess von
Dunkelherz, much against her will, to remain within
the mystic boundary.   Taking then a small packet
from his breast, he scattered some powder on the
ground and muttered strange words in an unknown
tongue.   Then arose amid the calm sunshine of that

lovely summer day the sound of rushing whirlwinds and stormy gusts ; a dark cloud intervened between the earth and the sun, enveloping all around in sulphureous darkness. When it cleared away, lo! high within the magic circle towered a gigantic pillar of smoke. From the centre of this terrible apparition gleamed forth two fiery eyes. A cold chill of horror ran through the spectators, though the air was hot and sultry.

Hyas now motioned to Bruno that his lips must ask the fateful question. The Baron, compelled to speak, reluctantly addressed himself thus to the hideous shape :—" Dread Spirit, whether of good or of evil, I adjure thee to tell me whether the Lady Alcyone has been true and faithful to me, and guiltless of the foul deeds ascribed to her."

" Blind mortal ! " replied the cloudy phantom, " pure and transparent as the dewdrop hath the heart of Alcyone been unto thee ; there breathes not on your dull earth a spirit more free from guile."

As these words fell from above, a low muttered growl of thunder was heard, while Hyas, turning to the silent, awe-struck beholders, cried aloud, " The innocence of my sister is proved by the reluctant words of Varishka, the dark genie, who could have claimed her for his own had her deeds been evil.

But, alas! I fear the dread witness has exhausted one innocent life in the fierce struggle."

As he spoke thick darkness fell upon them, and when it cleared away the mysterious shape had disappeared. The bright sun poured its health-giving rays again over the panic-stricken multitude, and a cool wind blew away the last traces of the awful Varishka. All eyes were bent on Hyas, whose beauty seemed absolutely marvellous, as, tenderly embracing his sister, he turned swiftly aside into the crowd, and ere they were aware had totally disappeared from view. Loud acclamations in favour of Alcyone rang forth from the changeful thousands on either side, as they swayed to and fro preparatory to breaking up altogether.

Bruno alone stood irresolute; a thousand conflicting emotions paled his usually ruddy cheek; but his wife's sweet voice called to him. He approached her; her face was full of anxiety. "Let us return home at once," she whispered; "I fear for our babe."

And well she might, for the fragile Violet lay almost lifeless on her mother's knee, the laboured breath passing slowly through her cold lips. They drove rapidly home. The Baron, full of remorse, would fain have thrown himself at his wife's feet, but her thoughts were turned only to her suffering child, as she at last bore it into the nursery, where in happier days she had so often lulled it to sleep. For some time Bruno remained beside her, and aided in trying various restoratives. At length, summoned by his official duties, he was forced to depart. Several hours elapsed before he could absent himself from the Reichstag.

A strange hush pervaded his home as he once more entered its portals. He gained the nursery door, and, pausing, gently pushed it aside. In the waning light he beheld his wife half kneeling, half lying upon their little one's cot. Violet's face, illumined by the last rays of daylight, was pale and peaceful. It shone with a solemn light—unlike, oh! how unlike, his own playful pet! Her dark blue eyes were heavily closed, and her little hands meekly folded on her breast. The mother's voice stole on his ear—" Fare thee well, my darling! good-bye, my angel child! but only for a brief space I bid thee adieu. Thou art folded now in arms that can shelter thee more safely from the passing blast than those of thy poor mother. I shall go to thee, my Violet—but never, never more shalt thou return to me." These and many similar words were poured forth by the weeping mother as Bruno unobserved stood silently listening. His heart felt ready to burst; it seemed as if some chord within him gave way at that moment with a throb of pain.

For a long time unknown to himself Alcyone's soft influence had gradually undermined his harsh scepticism. At that moment a ray of heavenly light shot as it were from the upward pathway of his dead child into the dark recesses of his soul, and with tender humility he knelt by his wife's side and placed his hand on hers. Startled and amazed, she turned and met her husband's eye : it shone with a new and softened light ; there was no need for him to explain to her what he felt. Over the death-bed of their fairest hope they for the first time experienced the ineffable yet chastened joy of sharing the same faith—of worshipping together the same unseen God.

At length Alcyone slowly rose from her knees, and casting a long, fond look on the lifeless form of her babe, she led her husband from the chamber. Together they ascended the narrow stair ; together they opened the small, well-known door, and emerged, hand-in-hand, amid the now darkened twilight, upon the open roof.

"Bruno," murmured she, "the time for our separation has come; you have declared your belief in the immortality of the soul ; your poor Alcyone, in the midst of her imperfections, has brought you one step nearer the gates of Paradise. I now return to my celestial home, but shall there await you, my beloved, in the sure and certain hope of a long eternity together unchequered by the sorrows that have assailed our path in this mortal world."

Thus saying, for the first time, the gentle Alcyone passionately strained her arms around her husband; the pressure relaxed, he tottered forward; he was— alone! A long trail of light shone for a moment athwart the evening sky; the peaceful Pleiades beamed forth in brightest beauty; he called aloud, but only silence reigned around; in uncontrollable emotion the strong man fell fainting to the ground.

How long he thus remained he never knew; but he woke at last to find the midnight moon shining upon him. He raised himself, confused and aching; he passed his hand across his brow—Was the past a reality? A tear rolled down his time-worn cheek which his keen eye had never shed, but it might be the cold dewdrop of the early morn. Beside him lay the coat and hat he had worn in returning from the Reichstag. It must be some long, strange dream that, coming on him exhausted and weary, had harassed his brain through the weird watches of the night.

As these thoughts coursed through his mind his eye fell on his left hand; upon it there sparkled a stone of extraordinary brilliancy, which recalled to him the gem on Alcyone's forehead. He strove to remove the jewel, but, though easily fitting to his finger, the magic circlet refused to be taken from its place.

The reality of the past then rushed upon the proud Baron's mind with the resistless force of inward conviction. Humbled and sorrowful, the great philosopher's wondrous attainments and mighty intellectual resources seemed for the moment to become as less than the dust beneath his feet. With the simple faith of a little child, he bent his knee alone before his Maker, and cried, in tones of repentant sadness, "Lord, I believe, help Thou mine unbelief."

ESGAIR: THE BRIDE OF LLYN IDWYL.

ESGAIR: THE BRIDE OF LLYN IDWYL.

AMONG the mountains of Caernarvonshire none are more gloomy and precipitous than the dark sister Glydirs Fawr and Bach. Towering sublimely above the solitary waters of Llyn Idwyl, they rear their proud summits well nigh on a level with that of the loftier but less rugged Snowdon.

Where is the wayfarer who can forget a calm autumn sunset seen from those barren heights?

Valleys far and near shrouded in dim purpling mists; shadowy gigantic forms looming faintly in the deepening twilight; rose-tipped peaks floating amid a halo of glory in the evening sky; silver streamlets breaking here and there in white lines the dusky shades below; while afar, in the distance, the broad slumbering ocean bids a glittering farewell to the monarch of the day.

Such was the panorama spread before the young Llewelyn many years ago, when in toilsome search after strayed sheep he came suddenly upon the high-

E

est part of the mountain.   To his wearied eyes, however, nature for the time had no charm.   With hurried
and anxious footsteps he leapt from rock to rock,
dreading to find some of his wandering flock with
broken limbs.   For, as with many other Welsh
mountains, the crest of the Glydir Fawr is entirely
composed of huge boulders roughly hurled together ;
deep treacherous crevices being often entirely concealed from view by the luxuriant growth of ferns,
heather, and bilberries, which yield most unsub-
stantial footing to the unwary.

Llewelyn's father, " Dafydd ap Gwynant," a well-
known chieftain, had been slain in battle, and most
of his possessions seized by his foes.   The widowed
Gwynneth, in terror for the safety of her only child,
fled with him to the wild region now known as the
pass of Nant Francon.   There in solitude she reared
her boy to habits of frugal simplicity.   As years rolled
on the widow prospered and her flocks increased.   Yet
still Llewelyn remained her only herd, and at eventide the steep sides of Llyn Ogwyn and Llyn Idwyl
re-echoed with his loud carols and joyous shouts, as
he summoned the cattle and sheep to their nightly
fold.

In these remote times wolves and other wild beasts
still lurked among the Welsh hills.   Nor did they
limit their ravages to the destruction of animals

alone, but when rendered desperate by hunger visited human habitations in search of their prey. Witness the touching history of Gelert the faithful hound, whose tomb is still to be seen in the little valley over which a dog's fidelity has shed undying renown. Hence the necessity for carefully collecting the herds at nightfall within some place of security.

Llewelyn at length discovered his missing lambs on the steep northern sides of the Glydir, and herding them hurriedly together, crossed the shoulder of the mountain and descended towards Llyn Idwyl by the rugged pathway which leads past the narrow gorge now known as " the Devil's Kitchen." It was rapidly growing dark as he reached the plain, and he was hastening homewards, when by the waning light he perceived the surface of that gloomy lake to be strangely agitated. As he gazed, the head of a lovely maiden rose above the ripples, and seemed to his excited imagination to regard him with a tender wistful look. He rushed to the water's brink, and was about to cast off his coat and swim to the aid of the fair unknown, when, soft and clear as an evening bell, these words rang through the still air :—

> " Three times lost, and three times won,
> Canst thou win me, Dafydd's son ?
> Tender must thou be to me,
> Tender should I be to thee.

> To my mate in bridal hour
> I can bring a princely dower ;
> But my wooing must be soon,
> Ere has waned September's moon."

Enraptured by these silvery notes, Llewelyn strained every nerve to listen, and as the nymph falteringly uttered the last words he felt a magic thrill run through his frame. He became possessed with a sudden desire to behold the entire form of the beautiful being whose head alone smiled on him across the watery waste ; but as he approached nearer the sweet face disappeared, the surface of the loch became glassy and still. The pale rays of the rising moon illumined only the wide level mirror of Llyn Idwyl, and amazed and bewildered the youth turned to his home.

After folding the sheep he entered the cottage. His mother had prepared a fragrant supper; but through Llewelyn's veins there ran a secret fire, and he turned restlessly from the food he was wont to relish in his calmer hours.

Gwynneth was a mother in ten thousand. Though she had wandered far to obtain the oakleaves over which she had slowly smoked the pink trout ; though her hands had been stung when she robbed the wild bees of their honey for her boy ; though when faint and tired from her long ramble she had risen with fresh energy to mix and bake for her son the

scones he loved; yet when she saw his disquietude
and lack of appetite, no murmur, no query crossed
her lips. Patiently she herself partook of the humble
fare, and strove to cheer her moody child, while her
own heart ached with vague doubts and fears.

Hardly, however, had she cleared away the last
traces of the half-consumed meal when Llewelyn extended himself full length on the deerskins at her feet,
laid his hot head on her soothing lap, and by the flickering light of the fire (fed at intervals with cones from
the pine forest) related to her his strange adventure.

As Gwynneth listened to his words the iron entered
into her soul. Every mother can sympathize with
the pang she then experienced. The child she had
borne through labour, sorrow, and pain; the infant
she alone nourished and brought to manly strength;
the all upon which every hope, every thought of the
future is centred—the widow's only son—the idol of
her heart—his love is passing from her. She is no
longer to him the first, the dearest. Dreams of a
nearer and dearer one are wakening in his young
bosom. The mother is now his confidant; but well
does she know that ere long the newly-beloved
will be his only thought; that into her ear alone
will be poured all the aspirations of his life. That
henceforth and for evermore the mother must resign
her son's heart to the keeping of another. Gwyn-

neth in that hour felt the cold hand of fate clutch
her past happiness.   Her pulse stood still.   But she
was a noble woman.   She knew the law of life was
resistless.   Come from a race of kings, with proud
resolve she nerved her wounded spirit, and casting all meaner thoughts of self aside, threw herself
with ardour into the interests of her son.

While Llewelyn described the events of the evening, the mists cleared from the past and his mother
dimly remembered an ancient tradition heard in days
gone by.   The half-forgotten legend ran thus :—
A prince of royal Welsh blood fell in love with
and wedded a water Nixie.   No sooner, however, were
his espousals accomplished than he, with his palace
and all his treasures, became enchanted and
covered by the waters of Llyn Idwyl, which then,
at Venedotia's dread command, rose to its present
height.   The water god, through the marriage-tie
of his beautiful child, had gained a subtle power
over her human lover, and despite her entreaties
worked this cruel spell to secure to her the unchanging faith of a mortal.   While Gwynneth told
this strange story, an old prophecy concerning this
very prince, which she had often heard in her youth,
suddenly flashed across her mind.   Surprised it
should so long have escaped her memory, she thus
recited it to her listening son—

" When Rhuddlan's child with man shall mate
A light shall break on Rhuddlan's fate ;
When thrice three wedded years pass by
Llyn Idwyl's waters shall run dry ;
But if that wedded peace be riven,
By blows at random three times given,
Esgair must seek her father's cave,
Nor quit again the gloomy wave ;
No slow revolving years shall wake
The spell-bound slumberers of the lake."

" My son," exclaimed Gwynneth, "all is now clear to me. The fair daughter of King Rhuddlan has seen and chosen you to be the deliverer of herself and her family, who once owned the greater part of Wales ; but who fell under Venedotia's spell so long ago that their existence is forgotten by the oldest inhabitant. I am proud that my child should aid in restoring our ancient line of kings. But Llewelyn," murmured she, placing her hand fondly on his brown wavy locks, "you must pray for strength, and enter on this strange adventure with the aid of heavenly courage." Long into the night sat that gentle mother holding counsel with her son, and even when they sought their rude couches but scant sleep sealed their eyelids.

Next day Llewelyn fulfilled his various duties with feverish impatience, he yearned for the evening hour, and as the moon's rays fell over the lone heights of the Glydir he stood once more by Llyn Idwyl's brink, and in a low clear voice uttered these words:—

> " By the Glydir's rugged side,
> By thy father's captive pride,
> By the strains of mortal love
> Stealing o'er thee from above,
> By thine own enchanted lake,
> Esgair, fairest ! hear and wake ! "

Scarcely had he finished, when a long train of light shot across the loch, and, glittering with a thousand watery diamonds, Esgair half arose and stretched forth towards him her lovely arms. A smile of hope irradiated her pure countenance, and as Llewelyn knelt awestruck upon the beach, she slowly chanted these lines:—

> " Through Llewelyn's devotion deliverance draws near;
> 'Twixt sunset and sunrise to-morrow be here,
> Though strife be around thee yet suffer no fear
> If Rhuddlan's poor daughter to thee seemeth dear ;
> Forget not that o'er her the sign must be crossed,
> Or she and her kindred for ever are lost ! "

With a parting wave of her hand Esgair slowly disappeared, and nought was visible save the reflection of the moon, which, dancing and sparkling across the dark agitated bosom of Llyn Idwyl, ended in a pathway of light at Llewelyn's feet.

It was an omen of hope for the morrow, and with joyful steps he returned to his home. Here, however, he was somewhat harassed by fears as to the poor accommodation they could offer to the bride.

"Dear mother," he urged, "she is a high-born princess ; her hair, neck, and arms sparkle with priceless jewels. She may scorn our lowly hut, and reproach me for bringing her to so humble a home."

"Nay, my son," replied Gwynneth; "the heart of a true maiden seeketh ever something more precious than gold or riches ; the love of a faithful partner is doubtless what Esgair yearns to find. It is, moreover, borne in upon me that the daughter of Rhuddlan will not come dowerless to the son of Dafydd. Be she poor, however, or be she rich, we will give her the best we have ; and I tell you she will hold it dearer than life."

Heaven that night shed its own peace over the widow and her son, and their last evening alone together was long remembered by each as a time of holy calm. By day-break next morning they were already astir. Many preparations had still to be made. Llewelyn went across the hills to petition Saint Tudno to pronounce his bridal benediction. The holy father was now making his yearly pilgrimage through Wales, visiting and cheering his feeble scattered flock, who clung fast together and revered with a passionate tenderness their few and faithful teachers.

It was at an ancient farm upon the slopes of Carnedd Llewelyn that Llewelyn and his mother had, only a few days agone, knelt and received the good priest's blessing, and Gwynneth doubted not that he would consent to partake for one night of their rude hospitality, for the purpose of uniting her son and the rescued Esgair in the bands of holy wedlock.

Ere the sun had passed its meridian, Gwynneth's hopes were realized. The venerable father, guided by Llewelyn, safely reached her door, and after partaking with them of their frugal noontide meal retired to rest a while, and to resume the devotions broken in upon by his unforeseen expedition. It weighed much on his mind that no church was near wherein the espousals might be celebrated, but he was fully conscious of the difficulties of Llewelyn's position. He shrewdly suspected that until holy rites had been performed the wild spirits would do their utmost to reclaim and recapture the newly-rescued bride. Ere seeking his chamber therefore, the good father carefully sprinkled holy water around the dwelling, and fervently besought Heaven's blessing on the approaching union.

Some time before the hour of sunset Llewelyn and his mother started for the banks of Llyn Idwyl. They followed the rocky course of that little stream, which still breaks in foam from the eastern side of the loch, and babbling and brawling flows past the very stones where Gwynneth's little cottage once stood. The evening was wild and threatening, and the sky had strangely changed since Saint Tudno alighted at their dwelling. Thunder reverberating through the mountains awakened hoarse echoes on every side. Wild clouds in fantastic shapes scudded across the lowering heavens, and fitful gleams from the sinking sun threw dark shadows across their pathway. Ever and anon drenching showers brushed by in short sharp gusts, half blinding them, and causing inexplicable terror to the ponies ; one of which Gwynneth rode and the other Llewelyn led for his bride. More than once, as they pursued their way, Gwynneth imagined that white arms and hooded figures waved defiance before her; but surprise and doubt held her mute, or perhaps ere she could speak the rain dashed on her face and she perceived that her fancy had conjured menacing forms from the eddying spindrift around. Llewelyn also was haunted by outbursts of mocking laughter, but when, amazed, he turned to his mother, the wild turbulence of the little streamlet taught him he had mistaken its noisy vehemence for sounds of demoniacal mirth.

At last they reached Llyn Idwyl's side. The sky once more grew calm and clear. The sun had long

since disappeared behind the dark mountain, and the
stars faintly twinkling overhead had already lit their
feeble lamps. The lake itself, however, presented a
wild scene. Furious gusts of wind agitated the surface. Sheets of spray bearing the semblance of
hideous figures were dashed hither and thither. A
rushing noise as of a thousand waterfalls drowned
every other sound, and Llewelyn in vain tried to make
his voice audible amid the din of the elements. Again
and again he endeavoured to shout Esgair's name, but
the mad roaring of the winds and waves was all that
could be heard.

"To your knees, my son, and pray for help,"
whispered Gwynneth in his ear, and in despair
Llewelyn sank on the ground and fervently invoked
the aid of Heaven. As if in answer to his prayer,
at this instant the moon tipped the frowning mountain ; her bright rays irradiated the wild scene beneath
and diminished in some measure the confusion and
uproar. Then, white and dripping as a storm-tost
waterlily, the lovely figure of Rhuddlan's daughter
slowly emerged from the lake until her feet were
visible. She advanced along the moon-lit path, which
alone remained serene and calm. On either side
horrid arms were stretched as if to grasp her shrinking
form, and rude blasts of spray burst in torrents over
her defenceless head.

Llewelyn knelt in silent prayer till she neared the water brink, when, springing to her side, he drew her tenderly on shore, signing at the same time on her brow the holy symbol of the cross; while wild shrieks and groans resounded across the lake. He lifted Esgair, trembling and exhausted, on the pony, where his strong arm was needed to support her. The moon suddenly disappeared behind a cloud ; the rain burst forth with redoubled vehemence, while such peals of thunder broke around and above them that the startled ponies could hardly be restrained from dashing madly away. Llewelyn, well-nigh desperate, in vain strove to recognize the homeward path. Black darkness encompassed them and hid every well-known landmark from view.

Just as he was at his wits' end, suddenly gleamed afar a small bright cross, shedding divine lustre through the gloom. At the same instant there fell on their ears the faint chime of distant bells—a strange unaccustomed sound in those wild regions. They paused not, however, to question the cause of the welcome phenomena ; but with gladness turned in the direction of the cross, which moved before them as they advanced ; Llewelyn still supporting Esgair, and murmuring words of encouragement into her ear. More than once he received rough buffets from invisible foes, and wicked threats were whispered by the

hoarse blasts ; but he kept his eyes fixed steadfastly
on the sacred symbol which guided them in the path
of safety, and ere long the unnatural tempest spent
itself. The fiery cross grew dim, and finally disappeared, and the rest of their homeward route was
accomplished by the returning light of the moon.

Nearer and nearer rang the joyful bells, as if
crashing forth a pæan of welcome to the belated
wanderers ; and what was their astonishment on
coming within sight of the place where their humble
dwelling lately stood amid unbroken solitudes, to
observe innumerable twinkling lights borne to and
fro, while, by the light of the moon, the tall battle-
ments of some huge building rose over the site
once covered by their happy little home.

Confused and perplexed, Gwynneth thought to
chide her son for bringing them the wrong way. But
now Esgair, with new life, sprang to the ground,
and, turning towards Gwynneth, said with exceeding
grace,

" This was my father's home. He bestows it willingly upon us—it is yours. But, oh ! take me to
your heart, and give me a mother's love."

Gwynneth hastened to alight, and clasping her
new daughter to her bosom, hesitated no longer to
enter the massive portals thrown wide open before
them. As they stepped beneath the archway, solemn

strains of music became audible. A long line of priests and choristers moved across the lofty hall within ; bands of fair maidens robed in white approached Esgair, and tenderly saluting her placed her in their midst. Last of all the holy Father Tudno drew near and motioned Gwynneth and Llewelyn to his side.

Deeply agitated by a thousand conflicting emotions, Gwynneth, Esgair, and Llewelyn now beheld before them as they advanced a small chapel brilliantly lighted for high festival. With slow and reverend step Saint Tudno withdrew within the altar space, and united in holy wedlock the strangely-mated pair before him. Long and lowly did they bend before the sacred shrine, and when at length they retired down the aisles, the clear high voices of the singers rang out in joyful strains, while far overhead the jubilant bells told with their iron tongues the glad news that the first bar of fate had been undone—the condition fulfilled that ran thus in the old legend :

> " When Rhuddlan's child with man shall mate
> A light shall break on Rhuddlan's fate."

Time fails me to tell of the splendours of that night of rejoicing, or the magnificent appointments of the castle. But it is impossible to pass by in silence the exceeding beauty of the bride, or the manly serious grace of her bridegroom. Esgair's waving nut-brown tresses fell over her shoulders, bound here and there by priceless diamonds. Her violet eyes, her dazzling complexion, her long robe of silver sheen, displaying every motion of her graceful figure, her wondrous charm of manner,—all enchanted the beholder. She looked and moved the daughter of a hundred kings.

Llewelyn's countenance, even in that deep hour of joy, wore the chastened expression of one who has struggled and suffered. In the midst of his new-found wealth he was fain to remember, with a feeling akin to pain, that this proud castle and all its appurtenances was the heritage of his wife and her father. But as Esgair turned her soft eyes upon him, the toils of the past and the uncertainty of the future were alike forgotten, and love beamed effulgent on his soul.

Night and stillness fell over that great castle. Only alone in an upper chamber—the widowed wife —the lonely mother—wrestled in silent prayer for her children until the day broke over the east and opened to the world once more the golden gates of the sun.

On the morrow all was new and strange to Gwynneth and Llewelyn; but Esgair guided them from room to room of the splendid palace, and related to them endless tales told her by her father, of what had happened within its walls, ere the spell of enchantment consigned him and his to the dark waters of oblivion.

To Gwynneth the long corridors and stately chambers with their quaint hangings of tapestry recalled her early home. Llewelyn (who though of princely race, had been reared in poverty) felt a certain restraint amid all this new-found grandeur, and bore with ill-concealed impatience the ministrations of the countless servants, whose presence fettered his free action and oppressed his simple nature.

Soon, however, the varied interests of his new position became all-engrossing. Surrounded by retainers skilled in every kind of sport, possessed of the fleetest steeds and truest falcons in the country, blessed with the tenderest of wives and mothers, he seldom had time to revert even in thought to the fewer and less luxurious pleasures of his youth. He and Esgair became passionately fond of hawking, and many happy days were thus spent, when, splendidly mounted and attended by a numerous train, they would scour the country around and return wearied yet joyous at eventide to relate to Gwynneth the adventures of the day.

F

It was during one of these hunting excursions
that Esgair, roused by the excitement of the chase,
urged her palfrey to its utmost speed, and distancing
all her companions, came suddenly to a small level
plateau amid the mountains.   Here a little streamlet
had its birth, gushing forth from the rock itself in cold
purity.   The hawk was already stooping over its
quarry, and Esgair finding herself alone, called re-
peatedly to the bird in great fear lest it should fail in
its object.   While she was thus employed, Llewelyn
came rapidly in sight, and riding up to her, playfully struck her on the shoulder with his gauntlet,
crying gaily, " Methought, fair lady, you were running
away from us all ; but you have deftly won the race
to-day, and yours must be the heron's plume."

The rest of the merry party now came up, but
while with eager excitement they watched the protracted struggles of the two birds, Llewelyn turned
his own and his wife's palfrey aside, and under pre-
tence of arranging her dress whispered to Esgair,
" Nay, dearest, wherein have I vexed thee ?   I was
only watchful for thy dear sake, fearing when out of
my sight lest evil should befall thee."

To his great surprise tears dimmed her eyes, and
the colour mantled higher in her flushed cheek as
she murmured in low tones, " You have struck the
first blow."

Amazed and incredulous, it was some time before Llewelyn could recall to mind the weird prophecy his mother had repeated to him. As they leant sadly over their panting horses by the little spring, a white arm emerged from the mossy bank and waved beckoning towards Esgair, while, like a faint sigh of the breeze, fell these chill numbers on their ears—

> " One blow hath fallen on Esgair's fate,
> And grieved Llewelyn's gentle mate. "

Thoroughly startled he rushed forward, but the fancied apparition was only a little shower of spray which, caught by the eddying wind, dashed itself over him, wetting his gay clothes and soaking him to the skin. Were the words he had heard but the offspring of his own imagination ?

Now with loud cries the victory of the falcon was proclaimed, and the gallant esquire, riding up to his mistress, courteously presented her with the heron's plume, and craved permission to fasten it in her hat. Esgair accepted the gift with her wonted grace, but it was with saddened hearts that she and Llewelyn turned homewards. The dispiriting influence soon communicated itself to their followers, and in melancholy guise the merry party of the morning silently re-entered the castle walls.

F 2

Ere they retired to rest, however, Esgair and Llewelyn sought the little chapel where their marriage
vows had been interchanged, and as they knelt
together in prayer an ineffable calm soothed their
troubled spirits, and on seeking their chamber a deep
joy cradled them to rest.

Their life now passed away in uneventful happiness,
until, as the time drew near the birth of Christ, Esgair
had a son, whose advent was hailed with universal
rejoicing. Llewelyn with trembling joy welcomed his
little child, and drew many hopeful auguries for the
future from his first seeing the light in the glorious
holy tide of Christmas. Esgair suffered considerably
in health, causing her husband great anxiety, and it
was some time before she could resume her wonted
place in the castle. But she seemed strangely
anxious to have her child baptized at the earliest
possible moment. They were obliged, however, to
wait some little time for the holy Father Tudno, who,
again travelling that way on his stated rounds, promised by a certain day to receive the babe into the
arms of the Church.

Meanwhile the nurses were forbidden to stray
without the precincts of the castle, and specially
warned against approaching either of the lakes which
lay within such easy distance—Llyn Ogwyn and
Llyn Idwyl. It was rumoured that strange forms were

to be sometimes seen wandering round the castle. Esgair herself, whose gentle ways had endeared her to all around, began to be regarded with suspicion, as, when hardly strong enough to leave her chamber, she insisted on taking solitary walks, was long absent, and frequently returned with traces of tears on her cheek. At such times she would redouble her cautions to the nurses, and sit for hours watching uneasily over her babe. They told wild tales, moreover, of seeing their mistress in the dead of night leaning over the little one's cradle and with clasped hands and streaming eyes seeming to wrestle in prayer with some invisible power. She would then clasp the infant in her arms, sign a cross over its forehead and replace it slumbering and unconscious in its cot.

But the slow weeks moved on, St. Valentine's day at last arrived, and with it the good Father to perform the promised rite. Every preparation made, and the little chapel adorned with the pale flowers of early spring time—the drooping snowdrop, and the Christmas rose, nestling in rich green moss from the glen— Gwynneth proudly bore her little grandson to the font, and the holy service began.

The wind and rain without, hitherto hardly noticed, now dashed with such force against the casements as to endanger their frail fastenings, while above the chant of the choristers could be distinctly heard the wild howling of the tempest. The little child itself moved restlessly from side to side, and seemed to feel an adverse influence threatening its fate. All eyes, however, were turned on the lady of the castle, who, with mortal terror depicted on her countenance, eagerly scanned the high windows and shuddered visibly as the storm increased. But now the reverend Father took the babe in his arms and ascended the steps of the font. Louder and louder roared the fierce winds without, and as one mighty gust shook the chapel to its very foundations, Esgair uttered a faint moan. Llewelyn impatiently turned for the first time towards her, and, angrily touching her shoulder to recall her attention to the service, muttered some hasty rebuke about disturbing the people around by her ill-timed fears. Father Tudno at this moment formally demanded the child's name, and Llewelyn gave him, as had already been agreed upon, the name of " Rhiwallon." As the holy Father, repeating over the infant the tender words of his faith, was about to sign on its brow the sacred symbol of the cross, a terrific blast shattered the casements into a thousand pieces, all the lights throughout the chapel were instantly extinguished, while a deluging shower fell on the group round the font. Eldritch laughter rang through the air, a piercing shriek was heard, and phantom forms tried to wrench the little babe from the good priest's arms. Undismayed and calm however, Saint Tudno gathered the helpless lamb of the fold still closer in his sheltering clasp, and ere the strife of the rough elements well-nigh reached him, the little Rhiwallon was already a member of the eternal Church. But in Llewelyn's awe-struck ear sounded these dread words—

" Blare wildly ye breezes a blast of delight,
A blow hath been struck by Llewelyn this night."

Now with flying footsteps came a page bearing a torch. The wild force of the tempest seemed to have spent itself, and comparative peace reigned without the castle. Within, the lights were once more kindled, but their rays fell upon a cold inanimate form. Poor Esgair had fallen forwards, her head lay on the hard stone floor, her hands were still raised as if in supplication to some invisible power, while dark red blood slowly oozed forth from beneath her luxuriant tresses. With a cry of terror Llewelyn raised her in his arms. He found that in falling she had struck against the stone step of the font, and a somewhat deep wound was made under her thick soft hair. He bore her tenderly to her chamber. Through the livelong night with keen anguish he and his mother (suffering no meaner hand to tend her) ministered to her wants. At times she cried uneasily for her babe, nor could they soothe or appease her until the little

Rhiwallon was brought and laid beside his suffering mother in the great state bed, with its dark gorgeous hangings and curious antique carving. Llewelyn, heart-sore and grievously conscience-stricken, bent over the half-slumbering pair. They seemed to his excited imagination like the flower and the bud rudely torn from the parent stem and fading before his very eyes. He listened anxiously over their lips to assure himself of their actual breathing. Esgair, half-awakened, moved restlessly until feeling her babe again cradled in her arms, she murmured low words of endearment over him, and sank once more into troubled slumber. Many days she struggled between life and death; and as Llewelyn kept the weary watches by her side, he mournfully remembered that it was his own thoughtless temper which had brought all this upon his faithful wife, and recklessly dissolved one more link that bound her life to his. She explained to him that her fears had been roused lest the powerful Venedotia should gain possession of their boy ere he was christened, and hence the strange precautions she had taken and her extreme terror in the chapel. She was unable, moreover, to warn those around her, as her first word of elucidation would have sealed the death-warrant of her babe; so powerful was the spell still exercised by the fierce enchanter over Rhuddlan's ill-fated race.

April breezes brought sounds of spring into the land ere Esgair, pale and wan—like one who has passed through the valley of the dark shadow—was once more borne down the castle stair and carried abroad to be invigorated by the reviving vernal air. She had taken a strong dislike to the "Castle of the Lakes," as their present home was called. Nor can this be wondered at, considering the baneful influence that had threatened not only her own but her infant's life. She entreated Llewelyn to build another dwelling by the sea-shore, where strength and health might more rapidly return to her, and where she hoped to be in a measure free from the fell designs of Venedotia.

With eager zest her repentant husband followed the bent of Esgair's mind, and, after many pleasant excursions to the neighbouring shores in search of a site, they at length resolved to raise the walls of their new castle in the centre of the rich plain which then lay between the proud headlands of Penmaenmaur and Penmaenbach.

Esgair took intense interest in the progress of the builders, who were now set to work with the utmost diligence. Throughout the long summer, she, Gwynneth, Llewelyn, and the babe with his nurses, dwelt in a little shieling on the steep sides of Penmaenmaur. Daily descending to the broad fertile meadows amid which was to be their future home, they cheered and encouraged the labourers at their work. Ere the mellow September time came round, the walls of the new castle had already risen to a considerable height.

It was now two years since the bridal day of Esgair and Llewelyn. Never had mortal man been blessed with a gentler, sweeter help-mate. High and low worshipped their kind mistress; and the most unruly of their half-savage retainers would fly to anticipate her slightest desire.

The little Rhiwallon was a lovely babe; healthy and well tended ever since his birth, his firm limbs and rosy cheeks were full of promise. His dark eye already beamed with intelligence, and his broad brow bore the impress of future intellectual power. What long hours that fond mother passed alone with her babe! At eventide she ascended the wooden steps of the shieling, and sending the women to make merry with their friends without, hungrily watched over her child. Gwynneth and Llewelyn perhaps sitting silent below, heard sounds as of a cushat dove cooing over its young. Sometimes the tones became more audible, and words could be distinguished—the mother crooning to her little one as if he could understand.

" Thou art delivered, my baby, from the evil fate

that menaces thy poor mother. Thy pure forehead
bears on it the sign of the holy cross. Over thee the
angel of darkness hath now no power save through
that mother's will. How could they think, my child,
that to save herself a parent would yield up her
darling. Nay, nay; when they tempted me to delay
thy baptismal hour, they fathomed not the undying
love Rhiwallon's mother bears her beautiful boy—her
treasure ! "

Such and other dreamy wailing words overheard
in the gloaming by Gwynneth and her son, revealed
to them the unselfish part Esgair had played in
the events of the past. Pangs of remorse again oppressed Llewelyn as he recalled his harsh rebuke in
the chapel. He now surmised that could the Evil
Powers only gain possession of Rhiwallon, Rhuddlan
and his race, including Esgair herself, would be delivered from all future trouble, and freed for ever from
the mystic enchantments of Venedotia. But while
Gwynneth and Llewelyn trembled at the danger to
which the infant had been exposed, they prized more
tenderly than ever his fragile mother, whose conduct
had throughout been above praise; and kneeling down,
they offered sincere prayer that through the exceeding faith and purity of Esgair's life she might, with
heavenly aid, prevent the sacrifice of her child, and
yet live to accomplish the deliverance of her race.

It was a lovely September afternoon, the sun streamed down on the rich purple heather, where Esgair, playing with her boy, sat beside a small rivulet close to the walls of the rising castle. The workmen, resting for their afternoon meal, were refreshed with milk provided for them by the kind command of their lady. Gwynneth, busily engaged in some labour of love, had remained up at the little shieling, while the solitary nurse who accompanied Esgair was seated with her work at some distance from the mother and her child.

Llewelyn had gone forth at break of day to hunt the deer, and as yet there was no sign of his return. A halo of sylvan peace enshrouded the fair scene and the actors therein. Amid autumnal silence the distant sea lay smooth as glass. Like a dim blue mist slumbered the far outline of the low-lying islands without. On either side rose the frowning sentinels of the vale between—the giant Penmaenmaur and the scarcely smaller Penmaen-bach ; while behind the smiling plain rose heathery slopes, undulating in successive lines towards the gloomy Tal-y-van.

Stretched on soft furs Esgair played with her beautiful laughter-loving babe. Sometimes she tossed him crowing aloft, and caught him tenderly again to her heart, then, changing from grave to gay, would whisper softly in his little ear strange old tales and legends. (It was afterwards asserted that when Rhiwallon grew to be a man many of his wondrous gifts came from his unconscious remembrance of that mother lore.) After much time thus spent in dallying with her infant, at length Esgair raised him in her arms and descended with him to the brink of the murmuring streamlet, being thus lost sight of by the nurse, who, still within easy hail, did not move from her all-engrossing handicraft.

The peaceful afternoon wore onwards, and soon Llewelyn, hot and fatigued, and with a somewhat clouded brow (for the day's sport had been unsuccessful), came striding down the narrow path, and, accosting the nurse, inquired for her mistress and child. The maid pointed out the course of the rivulet, and Llewelyn springing forward soon cleared the short space between, and gained the little eminence where the furs, still scattered in rich profusion, bore witness to the late presence of Esgair and the babe. Looking impatiently around in quest of them, to his horror and surprise Llewelyn perceived his son in the arms of a strange old man with a long hoary beard and white flowing garments. The little boy seemed pleased and happy; he was cooing to his mother, while she, seated on a rock in the midst of the purling brook, and within a stone's-throw of where

Llewelyn stood, watched Rhiwallon's every movement with keen delight. Llewelyn paused not to observe the majestic stature and noble countenance of the unknown (who was, in fact, the ancient Rhuddlan, the babe's grandfather), nor remembered till afterwards, when it was too late, Esgair's look of entranced happiness. So absorbed was she that she did not hear her husband's exclamation of anger, did not see his rapid steps down the hillock, knew and felt nothing till he roughly smote her on the shoulder and sharply asked what she meant by allowing their child (during his absence) to become the plaything of any old vagrant about the place, letting him also run the risk of every passing infection of illness. He would have added more bitter words of reproach, but as he spoke the old man suddenly disappeared. The baby gave a loud cry and fell splashing into the water. His mother at once caught and drew him out, and, with streaming eyes laid him on Llewelyn's breast, while around, above, below, with a sound of many rushing waters, could be distinguished these hoarsely-muttered words :—

> " The final undoing of Fate hath begun,
> And Esgair's frail portion of happiness done ;
> Arise and return to us, child of the lake,
> Nor nursling nor husband thy slumbers shall wake. "

Quick as light Esgair turned a strange look of

terror on her husband. "The waters, the cruel waters!"
she cried; "haste to the hills ere it be too late—hasten,
or they will overwhelm you!" No thought of her
own fate unnerved the heroic woman. Waving wildly
to the workmen, she bade them escape for their lives,
and indeed the nurse had already seen from above,
and turned to warn them of an impending tempest.
Lurid clouds veiled the sun, wild winds sighed around,
strange shapes arose in the bed of the little river,
madly leaping to and fro, while, stranger than all,
and striking consternation to the bravest heart, with
low growls as of far thunder, arose a huge black wall
of water in the distant sea, and seemed ever approaching nearer. Sea gulls and cormorants wheeled in
the air above, uttering dissonant cries. Affrighted
and amazed, the terrified workmen left tools, clothes,
and implements behind and fled in desperate haste
towards the mountains.

At this moment Esgair, turning, perceived that
Llewelyn, paralyzed with terror and remorse, could
move neither hand nor foot to save himself or the
child. Endued for the time being with superhuman
strength, she snatched the babe from his arms, and
crying "Follow me," swept rapidly across the uneven ground, sometimes stumbling and nearly falling, but never stopping to take breath until, on the
slopes of Moel Llys, she reached the trembling

crowd, who from this vantage-ground watched the
wild work of destruction below. Breathless and exhausted she flung herself down on the soft turf
and soothed the bitterly crying and frightened
infant.

Esgair's hurried flight awoke Llewelyn from the
stupor of despair. He followed and aided her as
best he could, and now stood by her side. In
silent awe that little assembly beheld the appalling ·
inroad of the waters. Like a dark pall, the slow
moving mass spread itself over the fertile lands
below ; ere long it reached the castle ; the unfinished
walls disappeared, and soon a wide watery waste
covered the whilome scene of busy labour and the
rich fields around. At length the remorseless waves
dashed unavailingly beneath the rising ground where
stood the trembling fugitives. Loud thanksgivings
for their safety arose from these simple pious men,
and they gratefully acknowledged the hand of Pro-
vidence in their wonderful escape from a watery
grave.

But now low sobs of anguish were heard, a mother
—like Rachel of old—weeping over her child, and
refusing to be comforted. The gentle Esgair, wan
and weary, lay prostrate upon the ground. Painfully she drew her labouring breath and strained
Rhiwallon to her poor aching heart. Her eyes were

mournfully fixed on Llewelyn, as if to take a last farewell. His grief could find no utterance. With gloomy foreboding he recalled the words of the ancient legend, and a cold thrill ran through him as he remembered that his fatal impatience had not only tempted Esgair's fate, but according to the old prophecy had .riveted still more firmly the spell that bound her hapless kinsmen; for was it not written—

> But if that wedded peaoe be riven,
> By blows at random three times given,
> Esgair must seek her father's cave,
> Nor quit again the gloomy wave,
> No slow revolving years shall wake
> The spell-bound slumberers of the lake.

By this time the tempest had gradually died away. A faint melody of unearthly beauty fell on their ears—as they listened wondering and entranced, they heard these thrilling words:

> Three times lost, and three times won,
> Thou hast wedded Dafydd's son :
> Brow that holy sign hath crossed
> Ne'er can be by witchcraft lost.
> By thy faith and suffering power
> Thou hast won the conquering hour ;
> Though the spell on thee must break,
> Rhuddlan's race from sleep shall wake ;
> Thou and thine shall dwell in light,
> Saved by glory infinite.
> Rise, the evil spell is broken,
> Peace be thine, and this the token.

G

As the voice ceased the sun broke through the clouds, and from his western declivity threw a long radiance across the calming ocean. Within this glittering pathway stood an angel of exceeding beauty, and of grave and majestic countenance. With his left hand he beckoned to Esgair. With his right he pointed to the golden rays behind him, within which myriad shapes of brightest loveliness seemed to move. The light fell on Esgair's head as she arose with new strength from the earth. Already a solemn stillness hushed the grief of her pale features and a new expression beamed from her pure face.

"Heaven guard and guide thee, my babe," she said, and placing him tenderly in his nurse's arms, turned to Llewellyn imploring him to wish her farewell. He approached and wildly cast his arms around her—the strong passions of earth still raged uncontrolled in his unchastened bosom —but she slowly disengaged herself from his despairing caress and hopefully trod the brief steps that divided her from the heavenly visitant. The angel took her by the hand—once more with overflowing tenderness she waved adieu to her husband, and ere the awestruck Llewelyn could move from where he stood, the red sun disappeared with a sudden dip behind the distant island. With him also, alas! were gone the last faint traces of that pathway of light, wherein had moved, but a moment before, those bright blessed forms, connecting earth with the upper world.

Breaking from his trancelike despair, Llewelyn madly rushed to the water's brink and again and again strove to end his miserable existence by flinging himself into the gloomy sea. But his people restrained him, and the nurse brought the little Rhiwallon to his side. The unhappy father turned to look on his child, then with renewed agony, as he remembered how he had for ever deprived that tender nursling of a mother's care, he groaned aloud and smote his hands wildly together. But now, through the quiet evening air —calm and serene—like dew on the parched and weary herb, was borne this soothing message from invisible realms :

> Farewell to the home of my brief mortal years,
> Farewell to the valley of sunshine and tears.
> Now over our castle on Arvon's pale shore
> The waters of Meinai shall surge evermore.
> Llyn Idwyl ! sleep calmly—thou desolate lake.
> Dark Glydirs ! no Esgair your echoes shall wake.
> But mourn not, Llewelyn, the fate of thy love,
> She smiles still upon thee from regions above.
> Arise and walk onward, nor idly repine,
> A mission that angels might sigh for is thine,
> To guide and to shelter through life's opening days
> Rhiwallon, whose future all Cymri shall praise.

G 2

The Spirit Divine hath inclined to my voice,
And parents and kindred around me rejoice.
My fate is accomplished—the spell overcome,
And Paradise opens to Rhuddlan a home.

The sudden shadow that had followed sunset now gave way to gorgeous colouring. From the closed western portals of the day emerged rich waving lines of gold and roseate hue, and spread far overhead. Behind the distant islands where the sun had disappeared glowed an atmosphere of living amber. For a brief moment the gates of Paradise were indeed "standing ajar" to receive the now immortal Esgair and her long lost kindred.

Awhile the watchers on the shore continued on their knees hoping once more to see that heavenly visitant or hear again the soul-stirring voice that had fallen from unseen lips. At last one by one they arose, and gazing seawards by the waning light beheld the broad band of waters still covering the fertile plains, the green meadows, and the unfinished castle. Little rippling waves broke at their feet and marked the boundary line, where to this day, the waves surge and swell between the mighty Penmaens upon the Cambrian Coast.

At this moment Gwynneth arrived breathless in their midst and joined her lamentations to those of the little babe, who, missing his mother, bewailed her loss in heart-rending tones.

The workmen now turned to seek a night's lodging where they could, for their temporary dwellings had shared the fate of the more lordly castle. Llewelyn, still carrying his child, motioned to his mother to draw somewhat aside, and as they slowly remounted the hill, frequently pausing to cast wistful glances around, and to strain their eyes in vain toward the fading west, he related to her the various occurrences of that fatal day and repeated the farewell words of his lost wife. " Hear me, mother," exclaimed he, as they gained the door of the shieling ; " by the remembrance of my Esgair's pure and holy life, I devote myself henceforth to the fulfilment of her behest, and while life and strength remain I promise so to cherish and bring up our child (aided by heavenly power) that he shall renew the memory of his sainted mother, and become the benefactor of mankind."

Clasping the babe closer in his arms he turned to enter at the lowly door, but with a cry of joy the infant stretched out its little arms, and lo ! soft and pure in the western sky gleamed through the dusk the gentle Evening Star. Then Llewelyn knew in his heart that his vow had been heard, and that an angel spirit shone approval of his humble resolution.

With mournful resignation, aided by his mother and cheered by the ministrations of the good Father Tudno, Llewelyn passed the remainder of his days in the careful up-bringing of his son. They never returned to the Castle of the Lakes. For at daybreak on the morning which succeeded Esgair's translation, a messenger arrived footsore and weary bringing strange tidings of devastation. As the last stroke of midnight clanged from the castle clock the whole mighty fabric disappeared, and with it the numerous servants, the fleet steeds, and the fabulous wealth which Esgair's bridal night had brought to Llewelyn.

Gwynneth and Llewelyn now fixed their abode on the giant slopes of Penmaenmaur, and often at sunset the father was seen pointing up the golden pathway and watching with his little son for the first pale ray of the Evening Star.

Rhiwallon grew and flourished apace. His was a fearless nature. He loved the sea, the hills, the birds, and the flowers. His childish brow only became clouded with pain or sorrow for the sufferings of man and beast, which even in earliest boyhood he ever yearned to alleviate.

When still an infant he was often found with a

sweet smile upon his countenance, and in after years could recall the dim vision of an angel form that bent over and lulled him in his dreams, but was ever absent when he awoke. Gwynneth and Llewelyn were long spared to foster his awakening talents, and ere they were gathered to their fathers the name of Rhiwallon had become a household word, for the sweet songs of the gentle bard are to this day remembered and sung wherever the Cymri tongue is known and loved.[1]

[1] Founded on an old Welsh legend. There is a submerged half-built castle between Penmaenmaur and Penmaenbach, which can be seen at low tides.

EOTHWALD: THE YOUNG SCULPTOR.

EOTHWALD: THE YOUNG
SCULPTOR.

IT will not surprise you, dear children, to learn that
after Hans Christian Andersen wrote his touching
story of "The Little Mermaid," the whole world
sighed with a strong desire to behold the true likeness of that loving and lovely heroine.

Painters and sculptors wandered anxiously by the
sea-shore ; not alone in Denmark, but in many other
countries, seeking thus to obtain a glimpse of one of
the mermaidens—whose whole race has been for ever
immortalized by the gentle Dane—longing to depict
on canvas, or to carve in marble, the fair lineaments
of the faithful sea-child who gave her voice and her
life for the Prince she loved.

Now for successive ages it has been well known
among the denizens of the ocean that trouble and
misfortune must certainly fall on the mermaiden who

should visit the shore too frequently, or permit her likeness to be taken in any form whatsoever.

Long, long ago, the most beautiful of the sea-nymphs rose in her gambols to the surface of the billows; and as in those days mermaids wore no tails, and were consequently unable to steer themselves properly, she was carried on shore by the force of the waves, where such was the confusion caused by her charms, that gods and goddesses themselves quarrelled about her, and artists in their enthusiasm neglected everything else to depict in all its bewildering beauty the sea-born loveliness of " Aphrodite." Great was the indignation excited by the appearance of this fair interloper in the aerial courts, and " Here," the Queen of Olympus, persuaded her husband, the awful " Jove," to issue a decree ordaining that henceforth and for evermore all mermaidens should bear long tails; thus confining their dangerous influence to their own native element; and furthermore forbidding them, on pain of severest penalties, to hold communication with the inhabitants of earth or sky.

Though centuries have rolled away, this dread command is still remembered and obeyed, and hence the extreme difficulty experienced by those whose artistic longings had been kindled afresh by the glowing descriptions of the sweet Danish writer.

One golden evening during the brief but glorious northern summer, the young sculptor, Eothwald, after a weary day of unavailing search for the far-famed mermaidens, threw himself down on the soft grass by a river's side, and lulled by the soft ceaseless murmur of the rushing waters, sank into deep dreamless sleep. As the drowsiness of fatigue wore itself away, he became gradually conscious of ravishing strains of music, and rousing himself half awakened to listen to the dulcet sounds, he still heard the harmonious cadences of some stringed instrument swell and thrill in tones of unearthly beauty.

Eothwald arose softly from his grassy couch, and stole noiselessly along. Keeping himself carefully concealed behind rocks and brushwood, he followed the sound, till at a bend of the stream he beheld the young river god Näcken, seated at the entrance to a grotto, playing and singing to his harp strains of heaven-born music; while, bathed in the evening sunshine, and with their arms lovingly intertwined, there on the surface of the water, in rapt attention, floated the lovely mermaiden sisters, Duva and Himingläfa, unsuspicious of danger, and forgetful of all else, for the spell of love's magic numbers hung over them and rivetted their attention.

The inspired Näcken continued his impassioned lay; the blushing Himingläfa, to whom his

song of homage was addressed, shook her long
chestnut tresses until they formed a veil around her,
and laid her soft cheek on the shoulder of the innocent Duva, who, childlike, wondered at her
sister's excess of emotion.

A while Eothwald remained motionless, overwhelmed by the beauty of the scene, but soon the
surpassing loveliness of the sea-sisters fired his
artistic mind with keen ardour ; he felt within himself that could he but reproduce these enchanting
forms in marble, he would die content. He
resolved to seek his home, and return thence provided with all the necessary materials for working.
He had noticed during his wanderings, not far from
this very spot, a cave, where he fancied he could work
undisturbed. The clay by this river being famous
for its plastic properties, it would be easy for him to
model by day concealed from all beholders, and at
eventide to steal forth unobserved, and gain new
ideas of beauty from the fair sisters now before him.

As he silently pondered and matured this plan, a
silvery voice was heard afar, and, quick as light, Duva
and Himingläfa sprang away through the darkening
waters at their mother's call, while Näcken, carrying
his harp with him, abruptly disappeared within the
shadowy entrance of the grotto.

Darkness came suddenly on ; the river, cold and

black, ran past Eothwald with sullen murmurings; the wild owl swept close by where he stood, brushing his face with her wing, and uttering her desolate cry. The startled sculptor well-nigh missed his footing, and only escaped falling into the stream by catching hold of the boughs above his head. But undismayed and undaunted, he groped his way successfully out of the wood, and then hastened cheerfully home-wards, light-hearted and content; for what were darkness, danger, or fatigue? The quenchless fire of genius burned within his breast; the long dreamt-of ideal was no longer a faint, far-off vision, but had become to him a reality of dazzling beauty.

Ere daylight returned Eothwald had been to his home and informed his old housekeeper that he was bound for a few days' trip into the country. He put together his working tools, and having at her earnest request taken some provisions in his knapsack, he swallowed a hasty meal, and before the sun was yet high in the heavens, was already ensconced in the cave and fast asleep in its welcome shade, after all the fatigue and excitement of the last few but eventful hours.

And now night after night, sheltered by brush-wood, rock, and fern, the enthusiastic youth engraved on his heart the exquisite beauty of those fair denizens of the sea; nay more, in the ardour of

. his pursuit he became himself enamoured of the lovely childlike Duva. Often while Näcken and Himingläfa held sweet converse together, their companion unobserved would float silently nearer and nearer to the shore. Sometimes she amused herself by twining long wreaths of the ferns and creepers which hung over the river bank. Sometimes she laughingly lifted small silvery fish from their holes beneath the bank; then remembering that air to them was death, she would place them gently once more in their native element, and smiling, watch their playful movements when they frisked around her, as if in gratitude, before they swam away. Sometimes flinging her long tresses of hair over the grass by the river margin, clasping her hands above her head, reposing half on land and half on water, she would lie with all a maiden's dreamy thoughts of the unknown future, her clear blue eyes fixed on the starry vault above, her every action a study of grace and poetry, until Himingläfa's soft summons roused her, when springing again into life and motion, the agile Duva excited new admiration in the sculptor's mind as with the swiftness of a startled bird she flitted across the water and disappeared with her sweet sister beneath the briny wave.

It is not given to me to say how Duva and Eothwald first became acquainted; but it is certain that before the young sculptor had spent many nights by the water's side, that innocent child of the sea grew to know what it was that made the long hours pass so swiftly to Himingläfa and Näcken, when they were together; for a feellng hitherto unknown sprang up within her own simple breast, and taught her to welcome with beating heart the appearance of her new friend.

What long happy hours they passed together by starlight and moonlight on that river brink ! How endless were the words they had to say to each other in those stolen interviews ! and yet, though all seemed so untroubled, a secret care disturbed the peace of either loving bosom. It is true that Duva had attempted to lighten hers by confiding it to her lover, for early in their acquaintance she told him that she longed to whisper in her mother's ear the story of her Eothwald, and to find in the majestic Ran's motherly bosom a soft pillow whereon to still the flutterings of her awakened heart ; but in tones of displeasure the young sculptor chid her childlike impulse, and went so far as to threaten that should she ever breathe to her family the fact of his existence, he could never seek her more.

Chilled and frightened at hearing Eothwald address her in accents such as he had never used before, the gentle Duva tearfully promised to comply with his

H

request, and to conceal from all the knowledge of
her earthly lover. But the concealment preyed on
her mind, and though in his presence she forgot all
save the bliss of being beloved, yet she had for ever
lost the joyous serenity of her early youth ; while
the very look which roused her watchful mother's
anxiety, gave her in her lover's .eye, a more etherial
air of languor and grace.

Eothwald's secret care was widely different: he
knew that his Duva might in some terrible unknown
manner have to suffer for his love; but his anxiety
was lest he should not succeed in obtaining her perfect likeness, and thence partly came his reluctance
to allow her to speak of him to her people. He made
sure they would remind her of the perils of holding
intercourse with mankind, and probably put a complete stop to their clandestine meetings, now only
carried on under the shadow of the more legitimate
attachment of Himingläfa and Näcken.

While the inexperienced Duva only knew and felt
she loved, the more worldly Eothwald gazed upon
her with a critical and artistic eye, and often sent
a chill of cold presentiment to her very heart's core,
when to her gentlest words he vouchsafed no answer ;
but, absently scanning her perfect form, would strive
to compare and calculate in his mind the accuracy
of his progressing model in the cave.

He found it easy to obtain Duva's compliance with all his requests save one; but it was for long in vain that he besought her to leave her watery home. Many a time and oft they parted almost in anger, and the poor little sea-nymph more than once weepingly entreated him sooner to quit her for ever, and go back to his own kith and kind. But Eothwald always returned afresh to the charge, for, besides his real attachment to the gentle maid herself, he knew that could he but once behold her fair proportions near him in the cave, he could successfully finish his now nearly completed model; and, by imparting to it those life-like touches which alone it required, he would be enabled to give to the world for the first time the perfect image of a mermaiden. With true artistic fervour he forgot his mortal love in the eager pursuit of his immortal art, and, brought completely to a standstill by the harassing intensity of his longing to have the living form at hand to aid him in his work, he grew so unkind towards Duva that with saddened heart the poor child promised to comply with his prayer, and arranged to accompany him through the wood the following night, when the yellow harvest moon would reign in her fullest beauty.

Words cannot paint the overflowing sorrow that oppressed the pale mermaiden's heart that eventful day as she joined her parents and sisters, for what an inward voice told her, was the last time. Old Agir, her father, gathered her to his bosom, and pressed his little Duva to tell her trouble, but with a forced smile she first nestled closer to that protecting shoulder and then sprang half sobbing away, and they thought she grieved over the approaching bridals of Näcken and Himingläfa and the prospect of losing her favourite sister.

The wild young Kolga blew through her shell, and in her efforts to cheer Duva made such a bubbling amid the water, that people passing in boats far above the sea-king's palace, paused on their oars to watch the agitated surface and thought they had discovered a new ocean spring.

Häfring and Blodughadda caressed their little sister and playfully asked her to choose whether they should all wear coral or pearls at Himingläfa's wedding, but with trembling lip she turned away, unable to trust her voice in answer to their laughing affection, and for the first time they deemed their pet Duva was sullen. Ah! how little they knew the aching throbs of pain that strangled her sweet voice and silenced their sorrow-stricken playmate.

At last the hour of sunset drew near. Together, as usual, Himingläfa and Duva rose to the surface of the darkening ocean, and soon were greeted by the entrancing strains of Näcken's harp. Slowly Duva disengaged herself from her sister's embrace and lingered long near the companion, till now the sharer of every joy or care. But time's relentless wheel rolled on, and through the woods by the river's brink gleamed the golden radiance of the harvest moon, as the mermaiden at length approached the shore where her lover kept anxious watch. With joyful eagerness Eothwald greeted her, and in low trembling tones whispered loving thanks into her ear; even then Duva would have withdrawn her consent, but the impatient Eothwald, without pausing, threw his strong arms around her, raised his beloved burden from the glittering water, and bore her swiftly towards the cave.

A feeling of deadly sickness came over the little sea-maid as she was thus lifted from her native element, but the soothing words of her lover infused new life into her fainting frame, and in safety they reached the cave, where Eothwald joyfully deposited his lovely charge on the couch he had so long prepared for her use.

Uttering but scant welcome the sculptor flew rapidly to his work, for already fatigue and exhaustion clouded the sweet eyes, that were wont to sparkle so merrily, and spread a new languor over the limbs of his exquisite model. With passionate energy Eothwald moulded his plastic clay, completely forgetting in his ardour the unwonted position of the sea-king's daughter, and her need of watchful tenderness.

A stranger in a new and untried world—a timid maiden strayed for the first time far beyond the protecting care of parents and brethren, the little Duva reclined amazed upon her fragrant bed of leaves. Strange thrills were sent through her by the strong night perfumes exhaled on every side from earthly leaf, tree, and flower.

At last she was upon that land about which from childhood she had dreamed, with an eager desire to explore its forbidden mysteries. But she thought not of these things, her whole heart was absorbed in Eothwald. The young sculptor no longer gazed on her with the melting eye of love. By the flickering light of the torch which shed its ruddy glow over the cave, she could perceive the artist's glance now fixed on his clay figure, now turned upon herself with a searching look of restless dissatisfaction due in reality to the shortcomings of his own handiwork, but which chilled and saddened Duva's sensitive heart.

Again and again the gentle maiden nerved her voice to speak, but faintness overpowered her, and a dreamless sleep already fanned her with its overshadowing wings. Eothwald's form swam magnified

EOTHWALD AND DINA IN THE CAVE.   P. 102.

before her eyes, and then vanished altogether amid the mist of gathering tears. The cave grew dim—the little sea-child again beheld the palace of her father—her lovely sisters waved a mute welcome through the changing atmosphere. With the tremulous sigh of a repentant child that has erred, but returns with glad sorrow to fling itself on its mother's breast, Duva, forgetting all save that joyful vision, stretched forth her innocent arms with a low murmur of tenderness, and a gesture of delight.

"Can you not remain as I placed you?" impatiently muttered the sculptor, as the sudden movement of Duva's arms altered her whole position, and lost irretrievably the graceful attitude he was striving faithfully to immortalise. Even as he spoke, something about his beloved alarmed him; he rushed across the cave, but ere he could touch her, Duva's fair form had disappeared—she was gone!

The red torch flickered high, and suddenly expired. The moon's ray, cold and pale, penetrated within the cave, and lo! upon the spot so lately pressed by the enchanting figure of the poor little stranger, pure and transparent in the silvery light, glistened a white pearly shell, while a tiny rivulet stole silently from beneath it, and trickled into the moonlit glen without.

Eothwald threw himself wildly on his knees, and

felt the couch all over in vain—in vain!—then in desperation he fled out into the wood and searched for his lost love, breathing her name in fondest accents through the silence of the night, but alas! awakening no response from the desolate solitudes around him. Wearied and heart-broken he returned at length from his fruitless errand, and sank into heavy slumber.

Hours had passed unheeded away, when with troubled recollection he awoke and sprang to his feet. Gradually he remembered that in his dreams Duva had again appeared to him. With bitter tears she sorrowfully told him that his own thoughtless actions had parted them. He first tempted her by mortal love to deceive and leave her fond parents and her beloved home; then as he moulded his clay from her beautiful form, in the self-abstraction of genius, he half forgot her sacrifice, and neglected her tender spirit. Wounded and unable to struggle against her altered condition of life without the comforting care of her mortal lover, she had fallen a victim to the law that ruled supreme over herself and her kindred, and lost her visible shape, which became again transformed into the water, whence it originally sprang. With streaming eyes she waved a long farewell, then, lovely as a morning dream, faded from his view.

Eothwald flew back to his work with fierce energy ; he felt indeed a high soaring ambition. He yearned to represent worthily, to this and future generations, the fair lineaments, the tender immortal beauty of the sea-king's daughter, who had given him her simple young heart, and whose affection he had so rudely requited. A solemn inward voice told him he had no time to spend in useless remorse, or in unavailing lamentation. Death's shadowy finger already beckoned him to the "silent land." Grief had snapped the first chord of life's hitherto sweet melody, and his days on earth were numbered.

He returned in a short space to his native city. His half-finished work was slowly removed to the studio. There by day and by night he laboured almost ceaselessly, and wove into a wild poetical dream the young life of the fair Duva and her family, as she herself in days gone by had frequently, half romancing and half in earnest, described it to him.

He designed a lofty fountain, and upon its six sides placed in groups of wondrous imagery her parents, their nine lovely daughters, and the young river-god Näcken, whose strains had first led him to his beloved. As in his lonely studio he ceaselessly toiled, he wrote down at intervals this explanation of his labours—that to all futurity might be known the names and history of those whose divine beauty he thus strove to commemorate.[1]

"Agir, the ocean god, who hates mankind, I represent in the prime of life, with a long flowing beard, which he holds back with one hand, in the other he grasps a sceptre. Enthroned on a gigantic shell, and planting his foot on a dolphin, his handsome features wear an expression of proud disdain.

"When the winter has passed (as our Northern poets have sung) and the May sun melts the ice, the ships in the harbour lift their anchors ready to sail, and only the wind is wanting. Thereupon Agir (who delights in punishing the pride of mankind by robbing them of their treasures—taking husbands from their homes, their wives, and their children, and drowning the mourners in floods of bitter tears) calls to his youngest daughter Kolga to begin the sport.

"In the next shell-like division of the fountain, I place Kolga, who, with short rough hair and hoydenish action, distends to the full her rosy cheeks as she blows through the valves of her shell a soft, seductive wind, sufficient to swell the sails, and tempt the ill-fated ships to sea. Above her,

---

[1] The description of the different groups represented on the fountain, is taken from a beautiful work of art, designed and executed by Molin, a young Swedish sculptor of great promise, now dead.

shrouded in her long veil, is the mysterious and
majestic Ran (Agir's princely consort, and the
anxious mother of his many children). She en-
courages Rönn, her second youngest, who gently
and dreamingly along the blue ripples stirs the first
breath on the calm waters. Häfring, Unn, and
Bylgia, with the little water-elves and sprites, help
to raise the swelling seas until the waves are mountains high.

"Then the hard-hearted and vindictive Boara (once
scorned and deserted by a mortal lover) crushes the
prows to atoms. She delights in the destruction of
human handiwork, and is therefore portrayed with a
sternly beautiful though cruel countenance. Next
Agir calls on Blodughadda, enveloped in her long
flowing tresses, to descend through the deeper waters
and secure the ships' rich treasures, for no lock or
key any longer protects them.

"But the fond father misses his favourite children,
Himingläfa and Duva; he loudly calls on Ran to tell
him where they are. 'Alas,' answers his queen, 'our
daughters are held captive in the web of Näcken;
up there, on the fresh water-stream, they float, like
one charmed, listening to his melodious song. I
have begged and threatened, but all in vain. Me-
thinks one or both of them is befooled by first love.'

"Then Agir arose in fearful rage, calling upon

his remaining daughters to entice Näcken forth from
the precincts of his grotto (which, being in fresh
water, was beyond the sea-king's domain) into the
deep ocean, there to take him captive, and deliver
their sisters from his thraldom.

" So they all float on, displaying their charms like
roses and lilies playing on the waters: their beautiful dishevelled hair, their graceful forms, their coral
chains, their strings of pearls, triumphantly making
sure of enticing the hapless youth into the salt waters.
But no sooner have they reached the entrance to the
grotto, than behold! a youth, divinely beautiful, is
seen.   Harp in hand, he sings a soft, melancholy
strain with the purest of voices.   The beauteous
sisters, scarce moving, tarry on the heaving waters,
and listen, entranced, to his heart-thrilling song.

"Awakening from his own love-dreams as he marks
the approach of Himingläfa's lovely sisters, the young
river-god sings of his happy youth, when amid green
meadows, and under verdant trees, he listened to the
melodies of birds, and learnt from them the sweet art
of song—until, restless and eager for change, he wandered forth from his early home into the wide world,
with endless longing for the unattainable.   To punish
his presumption, he was at length condemned only
to exist in water, and became the genius of running
streams.   Thus he pours out his lament in strains so

moving, that even the wild swan is arrested in her flight, and the daughters of Agir, deeply enthralled, heedless of their parents' call to action, remain motionless before the grotto, allowing ships and mariners to sail by in perfect calm.

"At length, Agir and Ran, angry and impatient, hasten towards them, when, enchanted like their children, by Näcken's exquisite lay, they also remain to listen, forgetful of the time and of the passing hours, till daylight breaks suddenly upon them. The relentless laws of fate forbidding their escape (if found within fresh water at sunrise), they all then become spell-bound."

Such was the description Eothwald wrote of his wondrous fountain, on which Näcken still dreams on, harp in hand, singing of the days of yore. The beautiful Himingläfa leans forward, modestly drawing her long tresses across her white shoulders, drinking in, with downcast eyes, every intonation of her betrothed. The child-like Duva, adorned as when the sculptor first beheld her, with long strands of priceless pearls intertwined on hair, neck, and bosom, raises herself from the water in the attitude he had studied a thousand times, and half surrounds her beloved sister with her arm, listening intently, as on that well-remembered evening, to Näcken's heart-thrilling music. No shadow of future sorrow clouds

Duva's fair brow; but moulded in all the fresh innocence of her dewy youth, she remains to this hour the
loveliest mermaiden that ever gladdened mortal eye.

The shell she left upon the couch of leaves, the
artist introduced again and again in his labour of
love, and indeed took from its shape the designs for
the six sides of his fountain, the figures on which
were the size of life.

At last the story of Duva's early life was given.
Raised from ocean, cavern, and grotto by Eothwald's
genius, her family were immortalized by his art.
The sculptor's task was completed. In a paroxysm
of agony, he fell on his knees as he realized that
though instinct with life his inspired work arose in
all its chill perfection before him, yet the living,
loving, lovely mermaiden would never more greet
him with her warm, shy smile, and her low, tender
voice.

At daybreak the old housekeeper came to light
the studio fire; for it was now winter-time, and the
snow lay thick upon the ground. By the first dim
ray of light she descried Eothwald kneeling before his
finished sculpture. Her heart misgave her; he was her
foster-child—dear to her as her own. She stumbled
forward and touched his arm; it was cold and motionless as his own marble figures. Then a loud cry of
grief told the tale of death. Eothwald was no more.

His immortal spirit had fled. Whether in the regions of the unknown invisible world he may once more meet and clasp his Duva to his breast by the blessed waters of Paradise, we cannot tell, but such may be the merciful will of that loving Father who watches unceasingly over the creatures of his hand, and feels a divine sympathy in their sorrows.

One of Eothwald's hands rested on the word Duva, which he had finished chiselling beneath his beauteous beloved. In his other hand was found, fast clasped— so fast indeed that they could not remove it from his stiffened fingers—a gleaming white pearly shell.

FIDO AND FIDUNIA.

FIDO AND FIDUNIA.

ONCE within a deep and gloomy forest there dwelt a lonely maiden. She had never known any companionship but that of nature, animate and inanimate. She loved the birds, the shy playful squirrels, and all the various animals, which having always known her there, friendly and harmless, regarded her in their turn, with trustful affection.

It made no difference in their feelings towards the young girl that she was not beautiful. Her thick sandy hair hung in coarse straight elf locks on her shoulders. Her skin looked rough, and her features were not prepossessing. But these poor ignorant creatures only noticed that her voice was low and exceeding sweet. When she stooped to fondle the frolicsome rabbits, or perchance to bind up the leg of some wounded hare, they thought her tender fingers wondrous soft, and her warm cheek felt very smooth to them as she pressed it against their furry coats, and pettingly coaxed them to linger a moment on her lap.

I 2

Strange to say, though the little maid had no distinct remembrance of human fellowship, yet she spoke in silvery tones a language which you or I, dear children, should very well understand.

She dwelt in the hollow of an old tree, and few were the wants of her simple life. A clear spring, bubbling up among the rocks near at hand, in the centre of an open grassy space, formed a natural bath, where every morning, undisturbed by fear of man, she bathed herself, and wrung the water from her dripping tresses.

In summer time she often slept high up between the forked branches of a mighty cedar-pine, where with sticks and long grass she had woven herself a sort of nest. From hence also she could contemplate the stars, between whom and herself there ever seemed a link of sympathy. To her untaught imagination it appeared that the heavenly luminaries were happy in being among others of their kind. Whereas, had she but known it, each one of those seemingly tiny lights glowed myriads of miles apart from its nearest neighbour.

Fidunia dwelt serene, content with her lot; yet it was only natural that in her maturing bosom the yearning instincts of womanhood should awake, and that she longed, with an intensity of which she herself was hardly aware, for some creature to whom she could recount, and with whom she could share, the pleasures and pains of her solitary life.

In the forest where she had her home there were no great alternations of heat and cold, nor was the length of the days so different as we find it in our own more northerly climate. Still it was spring-time in this land of which I speak. The far soft tread of summer already sent a reviving thrill through the woods and glades, and Fidunia's thoughts turned anew to her forlorn condition.

She remarked, as was her wont, the habits of the brute-world around. Every bird had its mate. The sober rooks perambulated the green sward in pairs. The thrush wooed his love in songs of gushing melody. The tender turtle-doves cooed ceaselessly to each other. The very mole that burrowed by the fountain side, brought a sable bride to enjoy with him the hidden comforts of his subterranean dwelling.

Fidunia sat and pondered over these things. Again and again she tried, like Narcissus, to see her image in the crystal spring. But kind nature, careful to spare the little maid a needless pang, ruffled the translucent surface so perpetually, that the young girl's face only cast a dancing shadow on the bubbling water amid the rocks.

Baffled in her hopes of even a shadowy companion,

Fidunia, with a tear in her eye, murmured "Alone, ever alone! Ah, cruel fate! How I sigh for something really to love me."

Awhile she remained motionless, gazing moodily into the troubled spring, but anon her quick ear caught the pattering sound of little feet upon the dead beech-leaves that formed a rich carpet near at hand. She thought it was the squirrels, yet theirs was a bounding lighter tread. She turned—and, lo! running towards her across the open space, she saw a beautiful dog. In colour he was almost golden; his silky hair fell soft as feathery down on either side of his little body. His tail and ears of darker chestnut tinge imparted piquancy to his shape. His paws were exquisitely clean, and covered with lovely hair. His brilliant dark brown eyes shone with extraordinary intelligence—at least, so Fidunia thought—as the little fellow slowly trotted up and stood before her, wagging his bushy tail.

"Art thou come to be my companion?" the maiden joyfully cried. In answer to her question, the small quadruped came nearer still, and very very gently laid himself down at her feet. His mute gesture was most expressive.

Fidunia surveyed him carefully, she thought she saw the marks of sadness in his wistful countenance—he gambolled not around her, nor attempted to lick her hand, but fixing on her his large anxious eyes, seemed to implore permission to remain by her side. Naturally fearless and fond of animals, Fidunia drew him upon her knee, and gently stroking the while his silky coat she asked him "whence he came, where his home, and what his name." The little creature could not reply in human tongue, but he continued to wag his eloquent tail, and to gaze earnestly in her face.

"If you are going to be my companion, I must know what to call you," said the wondering maiden. "My name is Fidunia," added she dreamily—but at this last word the dog sprang from her lap to the ground, and assumed a begging attitude in front of the little damsel. "Nay, nay, my dear doggie, I cannot call you Fidunia," cried she, but, after a moment's reflection, "would not 'Fido' do as well?"

Hardly had this name dropped from her lips than the wise animal bounded into the air, and then ran round and round in a manner most expressive of joy. Fidunia delighted, clapped her hands, and as at this well-known signal all her feathered and furred friends came trooping around to enquire her will, she at once introduced Fido to their notice, and an alliance offensive and defensive was forthwith agreed upon between the community at large, and their mistress's new favourite.

Ere long Fidunia discovered that her comrade was both active and playful, and though he could not speak her language nor she understand his, and she therefore never discovered his previous history, yet she surmised that he must have been separated from some one he dearly loved. For this reason she bore patiently with his occasional fits of low spirits. Soothed and cheered by her gentle companionship and thoughtful sympathy, Fido, before very long forgot his sorrows, and became the gayest of the gay.

Echoes hitherto unknown to Fidunia in the solemn forest, were roused by his shrilly bark of joy, as capering round his young mistress, they wandered together far adown those sylvan glades. Fidunia could now indeed venture farther from home, as however long they roamed abroad, the dog's wondrous instinct always led them back to the gnarled tree, the crystal fountain, and the green velvety lawn, for so many years the little maiden's happy abode.

She soon discovered that Fido was very accomplished in various ways—and she fancied also that he understood all she said to him—he watched so keenly every word that fell from her lips.

About this time strange dreams began to haunt the young girl. Night after night she wandered in regions such as she never remembered to have seen in her waking hours.

At one time she walked amid beautiful gardens— on either side of her bloomed a rich profusion of lovely fragrant flowers. Within each sweet floweret lurked a tiny elf, and as she passed along, fairies swung themselves forth singing through the perfume laden air in soft musical tones, "King Antiphates is blind! King Antiphates is blind! and the maid who alone can deliver him knows not her mission!"

At another time she climbed painfully along a steep path, leading through scenes perfectly unknown to her. The hot sun beat on her bare head, and she toiled on and on, ever ascending, yet never reaching the craggy summit towering far above. Beneath her feet, an unfathomable ocean surged and swelled, and broke in hoarse grumblings upon the frowning iron-bound shore, sending vast sheets of spray aloft, and awakening strange terrors in the woodland maiden's breast. White screaming sea-birds dashed around her, and as they brushed her face with their wings, she heard them cry wildly "The great king is blind, only Fidunia can deliver him—but she knows it not! she knows it not!"

Again the little maiden found herself upon a lonely terrible mountain. She stood upon dismal rocks whereon appeared no vestige of life. Tossed and wreathed in fantastic shapes, the very stones seemed to bear the impress of writhing agony. Though now cold and motionless, they had passed through the seething horrors of fire. Scathed and withered, repulsive alike to man beast and herb, amid their desolate clefts, only the slimy reptile traced his sinuous course; or the bright-eyed lizard peered warily forth on the shuddering beholder. Turning to escape, if possible, from this dreary place, Fidunia found herself on the very verge of a huge chasm. She felt a burning heat scorch her face, and penetrate her feet. Long tongues of horrid flame darted in lurid flashes from the thick darkness below. A sulphurous vapour enveloped her in its hot and suffocating fumes. She endeavoured to cry for help, but could not utter a sound—an echo like the reverberating growl of distant thunder filled the air around her with these words, " He will never see now, for the maiden dreams away her life in the forest, and knows not that she alone can save him."

From this last and most frightful of all her visions, Fidunia woke agitated and confused. Why were words of the same import evermore repeated in her slumbers? Whence came these awful voices that sounded through the gloom of night? Who was the Antiphates whose misfortune was known, as it seemed, to all the world save herself? It was early morn-

FIDO AND FIDUNIA.

ing as she sat up and pondered over these things.
Her feverish heart was refreshed by the dewy silence
around. Only through the trees came the faint
twitter of half awakened birds. The sky, brightening
towards the East, heralded the approach of sunrise.

Her resolve was taken. She would set off that very
day and journey forth into the unknown world which
hitherto she had only visited in dreams. She awoke
Fido therefore, and explained to him despite his
melancholy dissuading looks, that they must leave
the fountain, the lawn, and the tree, and travel far
beyond the forest to seek their fortunes among the
children of men.

Clapping her hands together, she summoned her
faithful forest friends, who sorrowfully accompanied
their beloved mistress and her companion as far as
their strength would permit, then bade them a
melancholy farewell.

Quite overcome by losing sight (perchance for ever)
of her sylvan home and her attached little subjects,
Fidunia that night sobbed herself to sleep, with Fido
in her arms, and half regretted her determination.
But in her dreams angels hovered over her, and
whispered encouragement to the weary sad-hearted
maiden.

For several days more the adventurers journeyed
through the dense wood. At night they found shelter

.in some leaf-strewn cave or upon some mossy bank, beneath over-arching trees. Then the innocent pair, under the protection of heaven, slumbered until day's reviving beams once more cheered them on their way.

At length one afternoon they drew near the out-skirts of the vast forest within whose mighty depths they had so long sojourned. The setting sun reddened the stems of the tall out-standing firs, and the scent of fallen pine leaves hung rich and heavy on the air, as they left the shade of the trees and stepped on to a wide stretching common.

Fidunia, bewildered by the apparently illimitable space before her, stopped perplexed and half wished to retrace her steps ; but Fido bounded on, entreating her by unmistakeable signs to follow him.

After crossing some old sand-pits, and scrambling across an expanse of furze and heather, they saw before them a small cottage; blue smoke curled cosily above it into the still evening sky; an atmo-sphere of peace seemed to surround the lowly walls. As they approached, however, a large flock of geese and poultry of all kinds, disturbed by their footsteps, made a terrible cackling, and presently a hale old woman opened the door, and came out to see what agitated her flock.

Fidunia, accustomed to the ways of birds, had al-ready taken from her wallet some of the seeds she was wont to collect for her feathered forest friends. The geese, well pleased, quickly gathered round, and eagerly fed from her hand.

Meanwhile, Fido gambolled up to the cottage dame, and begged before her as if to solicit her good-will. Thus, propitiating mistress and fowls, the little maid and her dog were kindly made welcome for the night by the ancient hen-wife.

Next morning, refreshed and thankful, they prepared to resume their journey. The good dame now asked Fidunia her history, and whither she was bound; the young girl replied evasively that she only wished to see the world, and was going with her dog to seek their fortunes.

" Nay, my child, that is not all," said the old woman; " tell me, I pray you, the exact truth." So saying, she fixed so keen, yet withal so friendly a glance upon the maiden's blushing countenance, that moved by a sudden impulse, Fidunia poured forth her whole story.

Her hostess listened carefully to her long account, and then resumed : " You have done well to confide in me; I am more powerful than my mean surroundings would lead you to imagine. I would fain have kept from you the dreams that have broken the peaceful charm of the forest, and set you wandering. I have, however, sisters who are

otherwise minded, and they (to work out their own
purposes) have sent these visions to harass and
perplex you. I was anxious to know how much
had been revealed, and therefore threw myself in
your way to help you. My intentions, however,
would have been frustrated had not you, dear
maiden, given me straightforward answers.

"The King Antiphates, of whom you have heard
in your dreams, dwells, in reality, in the great City
of Deva. You will come to it in time if you travel
along the high-road, which you can discover beyond
that clump of firs," continued she, pointing through
the open door to a little hill at some distance. "I
am unable to render you more assistance at present,
but if, after reaching the far-off city, you are ever
in great straits, take this crystal from your bosom
(where you must always carry it, concealed from
every eye, or it will lose its virtue); place it in
the palm of your hand, fix your eyes steadfastly
upon it, repeating, meanwhile, in a low tone, these
words:—

> " Strange gem ! upon thy crystal core
> I gaze, the while I aid implore ;
> Trembling upon the verge of fate,
> Oh point my path ere yet too late !
> I fain would gain the boon I ask,
> Is mine the strength for such a task ?
> Canst thou unloose the links that bind,
> Or vanquish powerful foes combined ?

Then, show whate'er there lurks of art
Within thine own mysterious heart;
On thee I turn a hopeful eye,
Bright stone of silence, make reply ! "

So saying, she drew from her own breast a beautiful sparkling prism, about the size of a pigeon's egg, and gave it, with some solemnity of manner, to her wondering guest. Deeply grateful, Fidunia threw her arms round the kind Anna's neck, and warmly thanked her for the precious talisman. With the good woman's aid she then committed to memory the needful lines.

When she had successfully mastered them, the old wife drew her hand across her eyes, and resumed, in a somewhat trembling tone, " I know not wherefore you interest me so strangely, my little maid ; but if you will be advised by one who has drained the cup of earthly pleasure to its very dregs, return, as yet innocent and inexperienced, with your faithful companion to the quiet joys of your peaceful forest ; nor seek, amid the busy haunts of men, those more exciting scenes where many a grief and anxiety must of necessity be yours."

She paused ; how could she cast a blight over the joyousness of that poor unsuspecting heart by explaining to Fidunia that maidens, plain in feature, and devoid of dowry, have oftentimes, from no fault of their own, but a sorry lot in this hard world compared with that of their lovelier or more wealthy sisters?

Clothed in her long, grey dress, Fidunia still knelt at Dame Anna's knee; the light from the cottage window fell full on her rough sunburnt face; her straw-coloured hair contrasted unfavourably with her dark reddish skin, and though her eyes were in some measure expressive of the gentle spirit within, yet their faint colour, and the absence of visible eyebrow or eyelash, detracted seriously from their possible charm. Her figure was not ungraceful, but her strangely-fashioned robes (which, prettily donned by some fairer being, could have given a certain *bizarre* attraction of their own) were but ill calculated to add comeliness to the young girl's unformed limbs and tanned though shapely hands.

As the compassionate dame hesitated, unwilling to speak too bitterly to Fidunia of nature's apparent injustice, her young guest laughingly replied, "Thank you, kind mother; but I could not now remain satisfied without seeking my fate in the unknown world. I shall never forget your promise, however, but seek your aid with this amulet in the hour of need. Yet," added she, "ere I and my dog leave your friendly hearth, we will do our best to afford you some small return for the hospitality you have shown us."

Fidunia and Fido, who had a thousand times alone together practised various little tricks, now went through many evolutions before the delighted old woman.

First, said the little maid, "What will you do for your mistress?" No sooner had she asked this question, than the dog fell mute, and apparently lifeless, at her feet. His stiffened limbs made it plain that he would willingly "die" for her dear sake. Bidding him revive, Fidunia then drew from her pocket one of the chestnuts she kept for the purpose. When the little fellow caught sight of this, he "begged" for it, but his mistress was obdurate. He then "jumped" high into the air to try and win his plaything; still in vain. Next he "asked" for it in doggish fashion, by loudly barking. Fidunia remained relentless. But now a sudden thought seemed to strike the clever animal. Raising himself once more on his hind-legs, he uttered such a tuneful howl—his apology for "singing"—that his mistress, with a pretended sigh, was fain to reward him by placing the promised guerdon upon the ground. Instead of rushing upon it, however, Fido, in an exceedingly graceful attitude, bent his head on one side, and gravely "considered" the desired reward.

K

His meditations coinciding with his wishes, at the
word of command he dashed nimbly forward,
seized the round nut, threw it up in the air, and
caught it again and again ; playing, in fact, by himself a game of ball.   Finally, he laid the prize gently
down at his comrade's feet to demonstrate that no
matter what he won, he would be content to surrender
all he possessed to her care.

Dame Anna, delighted with the pretty dog's
sagacity, caressed and praised him, and, after amply
provisioning his little mistress for the journey, wished
them both God-speed on their way.   She strictly enjoined Fidunia to refrain from mentioning this adventure, and advised her also to keep her dreams to
herself, and only enquire as she went along, for the
great city of Deva.   Leaning over her low garden-
gate, surrounded by her long-billed and splay-footed
court, the kind henwife long watched her late guests
as they crossed the bleak common, and reached the
small clump of trees which she had pointed out to
them as a landmark on their way to the desired
haven.

Soon after passing the summit crowned by these
few lonely firs, Fidunia stepped on to a broad high-
road, which she at once recognized as that described
by their good friend, and leading to the capital of the
country.

They now walked on and on for a weary time. The hot sun poured down its noontide rays, the dust arose in parching clouds, and followed with the wind their flagging footsteps.

At last they came to a part of the road bounded by a stone wall. On the other side lay a beautiful green park, stretching far away in upland slopes of rich pasturage. Fatigued and footsore, Fidunia and her little dog clambered over the fence, and composed themselves comfortably to rest in the soft grass. Sheltered from the mid-day heat in their seat among low brushwood and high overshadowing trees, they gratefully partook of the food pressed on them ere their departure by the worthy cottage wife.

Half playing, half teaching her faithful companion, Fidunia held aloft a little bit of meat in one hand, while with the other she bent down the branch of a neighbouring tree, over which Fido at her gentle command, bounded nimbly backwards and forwards.

Suddenly, a loud, harsh voice exclaimed, " What business have you here ? No tramps are allowed in my park."

Looking timidly round, Fidunia beheld a stout, red-faced, grizzle-haired man, in leathern gaiters, who angrily threatened herself and Fido with an up-lifted stick. Absolutely terrified by this, her first experience of man, poor Fidunia felt as if glued to the

spot. She could not move hand or foot. A surging
tide of red blood rushed over her face and neck, and
covered the poor child of nature with confusion.

Had she looked beautiful in her distress, perhaps
the rough proprietor might have treated her more
tenderly. As it was, increasing in violence, he drew
nearer still, when Fido, who already bristled with
rage, flew upon him, and ere he could lay hands upon
his trembling mistress, fixed his sharp white teeth
apparently in the fierce stranger's leg; but, luckily
for the savage Baron, Fido's jaws only met in his
legging.

Coward, as well as bully, the rough man changed
his tone and implored Fidunia to call off her dog.
Recovered from her first terror, the little maid
beckoned to Fido to follow her, and ere this selfish
squire could look calmly about him, she had flown
nimbly over the wall, followed by her dog.

They both ran a considerable way in their terror,
not knowing that the friendly Anna (in reality a
good fairy) had thrown so much dust in the rude
Baron's eyes, that confused and bewildered, he knew
not which way the intruders had escaped, but continued to search for them with wicked words and
impotent threats long after they had left him and
his inhospitable domains behind.

Meantime the travellers pursued their way until,

worn out and hungry, they came, towards nightfall, into a small hamlet upon the great high-road.

The village inn, with its gay painted sign of the "Golden Boar" flapping to and fro in the evening breeze, stood invitingly open. Fidunia approached its threshold. The spruce landlady, airing herself with arms akimbo at the open door, stared hard at the little maiden as she paused longingly in front of the steps. "Can you pay for a night's lodging?" she asked in a matter of fact tone. Alas, no—poor Fidunia possessed not one single piece of that hitherto unneeded money—without which she was soon to find she could gain nothing in the pleasant world she had so longed to explore.

She sorrowfully passed the cheerful preparations for wayfarers better supplied than herself with all-conquering gold, and heart-sore and weary sat herself down on an old stump of wood outside the village smithy.

Here, however, she soon forgot her fatigue for a while in watching the red furnace, and the grimy fire-illumined men who moved briskly to and fro, striking bright sparks from the glowing metal. They interested her strangely by their easy motions of power, and apparently inexhaustible store of latent strength. She was gradually recalled to herself, however, by perceiving that she and Fido had become the centre of attraction to a gathering crowd. The children accustomed to cluster round the entrance of the warm and busy workshop now turned their attention to this solitary maiden, and the beautiful dog, which, standing before her, ever on the alert, seemed ready to guard his mistress to the death.

The heated smith, coming for a moment to cool himself at the half-barred entrance, found an inquisitive group pressing round the young girl, regardless of Fido's low growls, as with hair on end and quivering tail, he prepared to spring on anyone who might touch or insult her.

Of a kindly and generous nature, and ever ready to befriend the helpless, Master Franz stepped up to the stranger and civilly asked her pleasure.

Fidunia, frightened, as well she might be, by the rude remarks of the gaping village girls, exclaimed in a tearful voice, "Oh, sir, I know not where to go for a night's lodging, I and my poor dog, we are travelling to the great city of Deva, but we are tired, and unable to journey farther this day." Franz, sorely puzzled, looked around in vain for help or counsel. He knew better than the shivering little maid before him what rustic gossip meant. A stalwart bachelor living all alone above his smithy, he himself, however compassionate, could offer no shelter to the poor wanderers. A sudden thought struck him. " Come with me," he cried, "to my good friend Dorothy of the "Golden Boar;" I warrant me she will blithely give thee food and lodging for the night."

"Kind, sir," answered the poor girl sorrowfully, "I have no money to offer to the good lady of the inn, and she has already bidden me from her door; but," continued Fidunia timidly, "I and my dog are able to make some few passes together, which might give amusement to the worthy Dorothy, and even induce her to grant us leave to rest for the night beneath her roof."

The friendly Franz chuckled with delight as he exclaimed, "By my halidome, damsel, thy words are well-flavoured. Dame Dorothy shall give to thee and thy pretty beast a hearty meal; and then, my mates," he added, turning to the assembled villagers, "we will step up to the "Golden Boar" when our labours for the day are ended, and see whether we cannot help the maiden and her dog on their voyage."

At these words Fidunia felt greatly comforted, and she and Fido fearlessly retraced their steps in the wake of the burly smith.

Dame Dorothy had long ere this left her door, and was now engaged in the great kitchen superintending with her own hands the preparation of a savoury pie, which somehow or other she hoped Master Franz

would that very evening help her to consume. Her
old husband had been gathered to his fathers many
months agone. Since his death the worthy woman
often felt the hours after dark pass very slowly. No
one knew this interesting fact better than the shrewd
yet simple smith, who, early or late, felt sure of a
warm welcome whenever he crossed the comfortable threshold of the "Golden Boar."

When the landlady heard steps in her passage,
a slight cloud of annoyance rose to her brow—
for what mistress likes to be interrupted in her mysterious culinary rites? The incipient frown, however, speedily changed to a smile as Franz's broad
figure appeared in the doorway. With a "welcome,
neighbour," she hurriedly stooped to shut the oven
door, an exertion which called additional colour into
her round healthy cheek.

"Friend Dorothy," said Franz, "I bring thee this
forlorn maiden; for my sake thou wilt refresh her and
her dog. I must away. I have a coat of mail in
hand that cannot be left; but anon I will return." So
saying, and without pausing for queries or doubts, the
brawny smith disappeared, leaving in his place the
weary drooping Fidunia and her little comrade.

Dorothy cast a keen scrutinizing glance on the
young girl, eagerly scanning her form and features.
Reassured by the brief inspection, her eye travelled

back to the polished mirror by the fire which reflected her own buxom charms. With some com-
placency she readjusted the snowy coif (slightly
disarranged by her labours), over her brilliant
black hair, and wiping her hands upon the rough
apron assumed for kitchen-work, she turned towards
Fidunia, and in no unkindly voice bade her welcome.

Nor did she do this by halves. She exerted
herself with real good will. Before long, rested,
comforted and composed, the little maid sat by her
new friend, and, while she fondled her faithful Fido,
she related her adventures (always excepting her
possession of the talisman and her dreams) to the
wondering Dorothy.

But now Franz, true to his promise, returned,
bringing with him many of the villagers ; for the fame
of the stranger and her beautiful companion haa
spread apace, and a rumour indeed had been set afloat
that the animal was gifted with supernatural powers.
Refreshed and inspirited, Fidunia and her dog went
joyfully through all the exercises previously described.
Besides this, she borrowed a kerchief from Dorothy.
She then put Fido out of the room and closed the
door, carefully concealing the white ensign in the
blacksmith's wide hanging pocket. She next called
her favourite ; with eager zest he burst open the half-
latched door, and ran round and round the chamber

sniffing in every direction. At last, after a long
search, he was successful, and amid loud shouts of
surprise and delight drew forth from the depths of
Franz's coat the blushing Dorothy's badge, the good
man the while looking not one whit more composed
than his hostess. Fidunia then neatly folded up the
kerchief; and Fido, bearing it in his mouth, lightly
sprang on the landlady's knee and placed it gently
in her hand.

They repeated similar tricks over and over again.
Hearty plaudits were showered on the sagacious dog
and his youthful mistress, who, flitting to and fro
in anxious excitement, and finding herself impeded
in her swift motions by the long folds of her grey
robe, drew them in a hasty yet picturesque fashion
through her waist-belt. Flushed and animated by the
friendly approval manifested on all sides, she now
stooped forward, wreathing her arms into a natural
hoop, through which Fido flew backwards and forwards with frolicsome ardour. Nor was this all, for
the trim landlady, in answer to an earnest whisper,
also rose. Clasping hands with the stranger maiden,
she soon learnt how to twist and retwist beneath her
own and Fidunia's arms in a quaint manner that
Franz and his comrades thought exceedingly bewitch-
ing. At the same time Fido, watching his opportunity, continually sprang between Dorothy and his

mistress, thus making a merry third in this pretty exhibition.

As they at last paused, exhausted and laughing over their own exertions, the swart blacksmith stood forth in their midst. In sober manly tones he addressed his neighbours, and gave them an outline of Fidunia's history, as he had gathered it from herself and from Dorothy. He explained, that she was travelling to the great city of Deva, but that, friendless and forlorn, she was destitute of the money requisite to procure for herself and her companion the necessaries of life. He added, that since the little maid and her pretty favourite had given them so much pleasure, he considered that it would only be making her a fair return if he and his fellows collected a small sum to help their·guest on her way.

His well-timed appeal met with an enthusiastic response. Grey-haired old men, tender-hearted mothers carrying their babes, blooming young wenches with their awkward rustic swains, all pressed around to deposit in Franz's cap their hard-earned yet freely-bestowed mite for the astonished maiden. The children whispering their thanks into Fido's willing ear, threw their soft little arms around his neck, and pressed their chubby faces on his coat of golden silk.

The bustling landlady meantime bestirred herself
and her household, and ere long set before the
company the pie she had already prepared, with
sundry enticing concomitants. Foaming tankards,
moreover, were placed on the board, wherein the
villagers deeply pledged the wanderer and her inseparable companion.

Overcome with gratitude, Fidunia could only
murmur half-inarticulate thanks to her kind friends,
as they warmly shook her by the hand. They patted
Fido also, as she raised him in her arms to conceal
her blushing face, and wished them both every success
on their journey.

Nothing is so alluring to a man as the sight of
the woman in whom his heart is already interested, engaged in works of benevolence and charity.
Dorothy's second thoughts regarding Fidunia stood
her in good stead on that eventful evening. Her
softened voice, as she encouraged and soothed Fido
and his shy mistress, sounded unusually sweet to
the rough blacksmith's ear. When she smiled good-
night to the villagers, placing the while a friendly
hand on Fidunia's shoulder, Franz, for the first time,
thought her face actually beautiful. Though no words
passed between them, Dorothy, when she laid her head
on her pillow, felt a glad thrill of joy as she recalled
the warm parting clasp of that hard and honest hand.

In long after years, when Franz and Dorothy reigned together over the far-famed "Golden Boar," surrounded by a blooming family and blessed with peace and plenty, the prosperous wife and mother, in the fulness of her joy, often wiped a tear from her eye as she remembered the true kindness first shown by her husband to the poor stranger. A kindness that had melted her own harder heart, and (undeservedly for her) led to the happiest days of her life. No wayfarer was ever again turned away from the open door of the hostelry. Heaven increased fourfold the worldly possessions of the honest couple who liberally shared their portion with the poor and the needy.

Followed by the good wishes, and laden with the unexpected gifts conferred upon her by her kind benefactors, Fidunia next day set forth once more upon her solitary journey—solitary, at least, so far as human society was concerned. But this strange girl never considered herself lonely while she had her intelligent though canine fellow-traveller. Now bounding far before his young mistress, now lingering in her rear or trotting quietly along by her side, Fido gave her an astonishing sense of companionship and protection.

For many days they continued to traverse long tracts of beautiful undulating country. At night they

always found shelter in some humble farm or cottage.
Constant and unfailing were the bounties showered
around the gentle maiden and her fascinating dog,
when in gratitude for hospitality received they went
through their performances together.   The money
collected by Franz was like the contents of the
widow's cruse.   As fast as the purse grew empty it
was refilled.

Fidunia knew not that her ill-favoured countenance
protected her from many a rough jest and coarse
compliment.   But it was so ; her modest demeanour
and unassuming ways rendered her less effectual
service in preserving her from insult than her want of
beauty.   Nor was the young girl as yet conscious
that she lacked those personal charms without which
life may sometimes become so bitter to the sensitive
heart.

During the last days of their journey, the high
road gradually led the travellers towards the ocean.
Fidunia paused, therefore, one morning, amazed at
the beauty and novelty of the scene before her.   The
road emerging from wooded valleys turned abruptly
to the right along the summit of perpendicular cliffs
some two or three hundred feet in height.   At their
base, the blue main, hitherto unknown to the forest-
bred maiden, broke in tiny ripples on the silver sands.
It was a tideless expanse of sea, and therefore no

unsightly marks of ebbing waters strewed the beach. Only a long bright undulating line showed where the unstable element found its limits and mother-earth claimed her own.

Resting on the bosom of the mighty deep, and looming indistinctly through summer haze, Fidunia saw the azure outline of a fair and distant island. There also, gleaming faint across the broad bay, her eager longing eyes at last discerned the white environs of the far-famed city of Deva. After revelling for some moments in the glad beautiful prospect, Fidunia hastened her footsteps, well knowing she had still several miles to traverse before she could reach the town, in which she hoped to sleep that night.

It was very pleasant to trip gaily along the grass by the roadside, with a lovely view before her, and fresh sea-breezes to fan her brow as she sped swiftly on. But as the day advanced, the heat grew oppressive. Again leaving the sea, the pathway led them by degrees from the midst of abundant vegetation into an arid and desolate region. Absorbed in hopeful musings, Fidunia did not for some time observe the change of scene. At last a sense of oppression made her look around. The stillness was frightful. No sounds of tuneful ocean saluted her ear ; no melodious birds charmed, as heretofore, the

wayfarer with their thrilling notes. All was mute
and silent as the grave.

Fido, with drooping tail and disconsolate bearing,
paced soberly beside her, casting doubtful glances
around. With a sudden shudder Fidunia recognised
some of the horrid features last seen in her forest
visions. Here were the wreathed and fantastic
shapes she remembered too well, the wildly tossed,
the bare and herbless rocks. There, as she doubtfully
raised her eyes to its summit (now visible through the
opening gorge), was a cloud of black smoke, issuing
from the very mountain round whose base they were
journeying.

Appalled by this vivid resemblance, and seeing
before her an apparently endless continuance of a
similar loathly landscape, Fidunia's trembling and
really wearied limbs refused to carry her farther.
Looking around for a resting-place, she was compelled to seat herself in the road itself, for a creeping
sensation came over her as she caught sight of the
bright-eyed lizards peeping between the rocks near at
hand, and surmised that the snakes of her dream
could not be far off.

Fido came and lay down beside her quite subdued, and she opened their little store of cold roast
chestnuts and other provisions neatly packed in her
wallet. While she was thus employed, forcing her

thoughts from the surrounding desert, by endeavouring to play with her dog over each morsel of
their food, they all at once heard the tramp of approaching horses.

Fido, though seemingly hungry, dropped his un-
tasted meat on the ground. Pricking his ears, he
listened acutely to the distant sounds, uttering the
while a low growl. Nearer and nearer rang the iron
hoofs along the hard metal causeway. At length,
sweeping rapidly past the corner Fidunia herself had
so recently rounded, she beheld a splendid cavalcade.

Beckoning to Fido, she sprang alarmed to her feet.
Forgetting in her haste the dreaded reptiles, she flew
quickly to the rocks above, where, having gained a
vantage ground of comparative safety, she paused to
mark the unaccustomed pageant below.

But a few moments before, the sun, shorn of his
beams by thick vapours belched forth from the
crater above, rode lustreless aloft like a dim red
ball.

Now, however, bursting through the mirksome
canopy, his rays fell with renewed splendour upon
the gay accoutrements and glancing arms of a troop
of mounted soldiers, whose advance was heralded by
all the merry pomp of prancing steeds and clanging
steel.

Fido, instead of obeying his mistress, had remained

L

behind her in the centre of the road, and now, regardless of her earnest commands, he dashed forward
vehemently barking.

Startled by the apparition of a species of animal
but little known in these parts (the few dogs in that
country being smooth-coated, and very different in
appearance from the long-haired Fido) the horse
nearest at hand shied to one side, and crushed
against his next neighbour.   The two riders (hitherto
sitting careless and at ease) thus nearly came together to the ground.   Enraged at this misadven-
ture, one of the men raised himself in the stirrup,
and with his long lance was about to make a thrust
at Fido ; but Fidunia, foreseeing her favourite's
danger, rushed down and seized him in her arms
ere the wrathful trooper had time to execute his
purpose.

This little by-play could not occur, however, without in some measure hindering the onward progress
of the whole company; and before Fidunia or the
irate men could utter one word in explanation or
abuse, a loud voice from the rear peremptorily demanded the cause of this abrupt halt.   Fidunia was
already escaping as fast as she could with her burden
up the steep hill-side, when another cavalier, of more
pleasing appearance, rode up and informed her that
"the King" wished to speak with her.   Reassured by

his courteous address, she hesitated in her flight, and finally remained rooted to the spot in amazement and instinctive expectation.

By this time the procession was once more moving on at a slower pace than before, and she now perceived in its midst, surrounded by the glittering squadron, a stately chariot, drawn by four grey horses, caparisoned in blue and gold. As this carriage drew nearer, Fidunia saw seated in it a middle-aged man of singular yet noble bearing. Impatience and dissatisfaction were imprinted on his speaking countenance as he turned fretfully from side to side. He seemed unable to notice surrounding objects, for his eyes, though wide open, stared vacantly into space ; while the restless motion of his hands betokened a mind ill at ease with itself, if not with all the world around.

When this gorgeous equipage reached the spot where Fidunia stood, the horses were drawn up in obedience to the signal of Domenichino, the official who had previously accosted her. Stepping up to its occupant, he now made some deferential communication. With a quick gesture, the King (for it was he) leant over the side of the carriage, and demanded, in surly tones, who and what had dared to impede his royal progress. While he spoke, his eyes gazed aimlessly around, thus revealing to the most unobservant bystander the painful fact of his physical defect.

Inspired with sudden forebodings, agitated by these swiftly following events, and frightened by the strange looks of her interrogator, the maiden knew not what to answer, but stood irresolute, holding her dog in her arms. Every eye turned upon her, and the King angrily repeated his question before she found courage to reply, tremblingly,

"Oh, sire, if indeed thou art the great monarch Antiphates, pardon the imprudence of my faithful dog: he comes with me from the depths of our forest home, where gallants and horses are alike unknown, and on the approach of thy proud train he sprang forth to defend his poor mistress, thus discomfiting in some measure thy brave men-at-arms."

At this curious answer, given in all simplicity, the soldiers exchanged doubtful glances, imagining Fidunia to be crazy for thus bearding their passionate sovereign. But the King hungrily fastened on her words. He threw himself from his chariot with wonderful rapidity, and, half groping his way, half guided by Domenichino (who hastily dismounted to assist his royal master), seized hold of Fidunia's hand, crying, "Ha! from the forest, sayest thou, and by thy voice a fair and gentle maiden?" Ere he could utter another word, however, Fido, already watching his stumbling movements with considerable mistrust, broke into such angry snarling that Fidunia, freeing her hand, stepped backwards, and did not see the gestures of merriment exchanged among the cavaliers around, as the unfortunate monarch spoke of her being " fair."

Though Fido's repeated interference was decidedly provoking, yet Antiphates preserved unusual command over his short, uneven temper. He entreated Fidunia to consider herself his guest ; to enter his chariot and accompany him to his palace, whither he was now returning after a noonday drive. She demurred at first, because of her dog, fearing that his misbehaviour might be severely visited upon him. As if reading the cause of her hesitation, however, and aware of her fatigue, Fido leapt from her arms, and, hastily flying past the attendants, bounded upon the carriage-seat, wagging his tail, and motioning to his mistress to follow. Aided, therefore, by Domenichino, she soon found herself ensconced in the carriage, opposite that great potentate, whose well-remembered name had first been made known to her in her dreams.

As she mused on his peculiar appearance, unable to discover, as he turned on her his dark expressive eyes, whether the King was able to scan her countenance or no, he bent suddenly towards her, saying,

"Maiden, I have more for thine ear than may be heard by others; meantime, I bid thee welcome to my kingdom." Ere she could frame a reply to this gracious speech, he leant back again and relapsed into complete silence, apparently absorbed in unquiet meditations.

The swift onward motion of the chariot was new and strange to Fidunia. Leaving the desert region behind them, they descended nearer the water's edge, and sped lightly along the smooth high road.

Smiling vineyards clothed the mountain's side on the one hand; on the other, the broad blue sea stretched her "ample field." The jangling of the military trappings gave forth a sound not unpleasing to the ear, as the escort swept merrily on.

Weary with her exertions, and lulled by the monotonous movement of the carriage, Fidunia half slumbered as she leant back on the luxurious cushions, her mind filled with youth's vague ecstatic visions of future happiness. But Fido, wary and watchful, folded lovingly in his mistress's arms, turned a vigilant eye alternately upon the uneasy King and his glittering body-guard.

It would be impossible adequately to describe the forlorn condition of the monarch, in whose stately equipage destiny had thus strangely placed the forest maiden and her dog. Surrounded by all the pomp and wealth of his splendid court, he was yet debarred by his misfortune from enjoying the visible beauties of nature, or the works of art with which his palace and kingdom abounded.

Unable to employ his powerful mind in perusing the records of the past, or the writings of the poets and philosophers of his own day, incapable of discerning the commonest objects in the world around, and conscious only of a difference between light and darkness, night and day, the great King's melancholy affliction demanded double commiseration in an age when comforts for the blind had neither been invented nor studied.

Music became a source of constant pleasure to him ; nor was it surprising that he invariably judged people by their voices as they spoke or sung before him, forming in this unusual way a wonderfully accurate conception of character.

It is needless to say that remedies of all sorts had been tried upon the eyes of the hapless monarch. Many physicians had exerted their utmost skill in endeavouring to ameliorate his condition. He had visited in turn not only the most celebrated baths and watering-places, but also the various oracles then existing in Europe.

Disheartened and hopeless, he had at last well-nigh succumbed to his fate, when a strange incident once more roused the seemingly subdued, yet ever dormant passion of hope in his breast.

Antiphon (the foster-brother of the blind King), while wandering on the hills surrounding Deva, in his vocation of shepherd, noticed sulphureous fumes issuing from a cleft he had never before observed in the mountain's side. Taking with him a torch, he cautiously entered the yawning aperture, and groped his way along, until he suddenly found himself in a lofty subterranean cave. In the centre of this cave lay a marble block, fashioned like a huge coffin. Antiphon hastened home to tell his neighbours of his discovery and to gain assistance. Returning to the cave, he and his fellows succeeded in pushing off the ponderous lid, which fell crashing to the ground, and broke into a thousand pieces.

Within the sarcophagus was now exposed to view a shrivelled though perfect mummy ; and an old man of the party recollected having heard an ancient prophecy which foretold that answers regarding future events should one day issue from " withered lips, dumb with the silence of ages, and awful in their semblance to humanity."

Antiphon at once carried the news of this prophecy to King Antiphates, who, ready to do anything to vary the horrors of his solitary existence, though secretly doubting the efficacy of such attempts, disguised himself as a shepherd, and, unknown to his courtiers, accompanied his foster-brother to the cave.

Here, after observing the accustomed ceremonies of purification and prayer, Antiphates approached the sarcophagus, and kneeling beside it, craved some knowledge of his future fate, humbly demanding at the same time whether any sacrifice on his part would procure for him the priceless gift of sight.

Having made these inquiries, the reluctant monarch, had now to lay low his kingly head upon the breast of the long dead, and thus in a stifling and constrained attitude await the much-desired response. Each moment seemed an age to the afflicted prince. All alone with these terrible emblems of mortality (for Antiphon remained without to guard the entrance of the cave) he listened for he knew not what.

At last there arose upon the still dank air, as if from echoing vaults beneath, an unearthly monotonous voice, chanting slowly the following words :

> A mighty King is blind,
> And severed from his kind ;
> In his proud breast broods dark unrest,
> No solace can he find.
>
> The lands he calls his own,
> His kingdom and his throne,
> Are his by right ; yet that fair sight
> Is kept from him alone.

Revolving decades pass,
All flesh, we know, is grass ;
With whitening hair, the king sits there,
He groweth old alas !

No joys of life are his,
He tastes no wedded bliss ;
A monarch born, a man forlorn,
Nor wife nor babe to kiss.

Far, 'mid the forest drear,
A maiden without peer
His fate shall hear, and wake with fear
From dreams of little cheer.

By long and lonesome way
Two loving hearts shall stray,
That sovereign blind, in haste to find,
And Fate's behest obey.

Yet guard thyself, oh king !
Lest kindness sorrow bring !
Forbear to love, or time shall prove
That joy may hide a sting.

That pearl—a woman's love—
Might angels' envy move,
But powers that be, in wonder see,
How mortals changeful prove.

Joyous and fancy-free
Then let the maiden be,
Nor teach that child from regions wild
The meed of misery.
But if thou dost, thine own the cost,
And woe shall fall on thee !

The hollow voice ceased, once more all was still. Antiphates in vain asked other questions, and listened impatiently for further replies. Meeting with no more response, and thoroughly exhausted by the foul atmosphere, he hailed his foster-brother, and, aided by him, breathed again with thankfulness the pure outer air.

They returned to the palace in silence, for Antiphates, proud and reserved, vouchsafed no hint of the mysterious words to which he had listened. He had indeed ample food left him for meditation.

This visit to the mummy took place during the night, and the disguised King passed and repassed his unslumbering sentinels by means of his own signet-ring, occasionally entrusted by him to confidential emissaries.

The apt rhymes he had heard haunted him incessantly. The mere mention of a forest was extraordinary—for with the exception of a fair-sized plantation in the midst of which Castle Xylina (the king's summer palace) stood, no large wood of any kind existed within many miles of his capital.

As to love, the poor benighted King knew little about the capricious god, save what he gathered from the songs of the minstrels and troubadours, birds of passage who, ever certain of kind welcome and liberal patronage, flocked in numbers to his court.

Unwilling to display his infirmity unnecessarily, Antiphates kept himself aloof in general from his people. His palace was indeed the resort of all the most talented and intellectual men of the day. His feasts were celebrated for the brilliant conversation and witty repartee in which, not only his guests, but the monarch himself, occasionally indulged ; at the expense of many an aching hour of lonely reaction.

But at these banquets no ladies were present, nor had the isolated sovereign any opportunity of becoming intimately acquainted with his fairer subjects. There were, it is true, the singing-girls, who nightly performed before him with guitars and cymbals, and gave the blind king some of the happiest hours of his life. Though he could not see their graceful forms as they gaily danced to their own music, yet the tinkling of the silver bells on their arms and ankles formed a rhythmical and tuneful accompaniment to their melodious voices, that wafted fourfold enjoyment to the listening monarch. He showered generous gifts on these damsels, each of whom he knew apart by her voice and step. They were, however, but the toys of the hour.

When in pomp and state the King went abroad in his chariot, his fair subjects anxiously pressed together to catch a glimpse of their sovereign's stern yet handsome features ; but though they gratified their own curiosity, no reciprocal vision of bewildering charms crossed the darkened vision of their lonely prince, as he was whirled proudly by in his dazzling equipage.

Unwonted feelings therefore stirred in Antiphates' bosom as the prophecy of the cave again and again rang through his mind. After several days spent in musing and reflection, he resolved to return to the oracle, and demand more exact particulars concerning the forest maiden and the " two loving hearts " mentioned, anxious to set forth in pursuit of them, if need be, round the world.

Antiphon therefore, favoured by the darkness, once more led his royal foster-brother to the mountain side, but no cave could they discover, though for several hours they wandered up and down the very spot where the shepherd had carefully noted the entrance by certain landmarks.

Irritated and disappointed, Antiphates at last gave up the useless search, and during the succeeding days busied himself in sending forth express couriers over the country, north, west, and east, to seek for the forest, and to find out and bring to Deva all discoverable denizens of woods, forests, and thickets. Besides this, he issued a royal mandate, setting forth that every wandering maiden should instantly be conducted to his palace. A few strolling gipsies were in consequence brought before him, and told innumerable falsehoods concerning their previous lives and companions, but none of them were able to throw the least light upon the cause of the King's defective eyesight.

Pending the result of more active measures, however, Antiphates was roused from the apathy into which he had been plunged for many years regarding his misfortune, and taught himself to hope he hardly knew what, from the hidden pages of the future. But day after day went by, and no fresh event enlivened the dismal tranquillity of the palace precincts.

We may thus more readily understand the monarch's abrupt condescension and excitement on hearing Fidunia's first words, and learning that she had but lately quitted a forest. Her sweetly modulated voice at once carried a favourable impression to his sensitive ear, and, conjoined with the mysterious and ever-present prophecy, touched a slumbering chord in his jaded breast.

Indeed, as they now drove back to the city from whence he had issued so short a time before in listless uncertainty, his mind ran riot with wild chaotic fancies.

They drew near the frowning gates of Deva. A sudden pause, as the massive portals rolled back on their hinges, and the soldiers presented arms, awoke Fidunia from her trance. She started and looked around, eagerly surveying the splendours of that enchanting capital.

Meanwhile the fairer inhabitants of the town gathering, according to primeval custom, by balcony, window, and doorway, to feast their eyes on the royal pageant and the gallant escort of cavaliers; passed from mouth to mouth the incredible news that a stranger damsel was seated in their monarch's chariot. Ere the gaping crowd had time, however, to note more than the mere outline of a drooping form, the narrow streets were swiftly threaded, and scaling the little hill on which Xylina stood, the whole squadron disappeared within the leafy boundaries of King Antiphates' summer residence.

Fidunia could not repress an exclamation of delighted wonder as they halted at the palace door.

Castle Xylina rose in turreted heights of dazzling whiteness above them, pure as the day it was completed. In that favoured climate neither smoke nor inclement weather marred the snowy beauties of its marble walls and terraces. It was approached by seven broad alleys: six of these, carpeted with natural greensward, converged through the small wood already mentioned, towards the broad central plateau. The seventh avenue, leading from the town, up which the King had just driven, was like the city itself, paved with lava.

The castle from its elevated situation, commanded an exquisite prospect towards the south across the open bay of Deva. The surrounding trees completely shut out the neighbouring town. Only faint, distant sounds, and the chiming of church and convent bells borne upon the air, betokened the near presence of the busy thousands below. Innumerable craft, moreover, moored or moving on the still blue waters, gave an air of life to the otherwise dreamy silence, that with mistlike wings enfolded the fair prosperous Deva and her environs as Fidunia thus first beheld them.

But now a courtly throng pressed around, a hundred eyes were bent on the embarrassed stranger and her singular companion, a hundred hands outstretched to assist her in her descent from the carriage. But no sooner had the King himself touched the ground in safety, than he turned, and taking her hand in his, led her slowly up the broad white marble steps into the central ·hall of his magnificent palace.

She had scarcely time to glance round her ere her royal host, divining both her fatigue and her bashfulness, summoned and gave minute directions to the women of the palace regarding her welfare, and resigned her into their charge. Smiling kindly on their unexpected guest, they ushered her along lofty passages to a chamber widely different from any the simple maiden had ever beheld either in her wanderings or even in her dreams.

Thoroughly overcome by fatigue, and hardly pausing even to partake of the tempting fare presented to her, or to survey the beauties of her new abode, Fidunia sought her pillow. The neat-handed abigails, after preparing a bed for Fido within the recess where stood his mistress's couch, retired, first bidding her summon them at will, as their apartments were close at hand.

Youth and exhaustion soon closed the stranger's eyes, and it was late on the following day before Fidunia could rouse herself completely from her heavy slumbers.

At length a continuous plashing sound mingled itself with her dreams. She thought she was once more in her forest home, and that the little fountain with its clear bubbling waters invited her to her morning bath.

She slowly unclosed her eyes. But no leafy branches spread their matted foliage above her head ; lovely rosy curtains fell instead on either side of her soft little couch. She raised herself—surprised and wondering—at her first movement, Fido already on the alert, capered across the tesselated floor, oddly slipping hither and thither on its smooth surface.

M

She stepped carefully from her alcove, and proceeded on a voyage of exploration.   She soon ascertained that the sound of running water was no vain
product of her own imagination, but that it came
from a recess corresponding to that in which she had
slept.   Within this niche a marble Triton poured
through his conch-shell a continuous stream.   On
either side the entrance to the snowy basin beneath,
a nymph so stood that the roseate curtains could
either be held back in their extended arms, or loosened
completely to shut off the recess from the rest of the
room.

Overjoyed at discovering this welcome substitute
for her oft-regretted forest spring, Fidunia swiftly
performed her simple toilet.

With all the carelessness of one little accustomed
to regard her personal appearance, she hardly even
glanced at the magnificent burnished mirror and its
costly accessories, but hastened from window to
window, eager to become acquainted with her new
abode.

Towards the south, connected outside by a shady
verandah, three long windows fronted the open bay,
commanding the same extensive view that had delighted her the evening before.   Two of similar form
opened eastward, and Fidunia could scarcely repress
a shudder, as raising her eyes to scan the more

distant horizon, she beheld, frowning behind nearer slopes of verdant loveliness, the grim mountain of her dreams, whose gloomy boundaries she had skirted on the previous day. A slumberous cloud partially shrouded its dark heights. In the vista of coast, cape, and blue headland lengthening beyond, earth, sea, and sky, melted into one indistinguishable haze of atmospheric beauty.

Easily unfastening one of these eastern windows, Fidunia perceived a flight of steps leading thence into the palace gardens below. Followed by Fido, the fearless child of nature quickly descended the stairs, and plunged into the artificial intricacies of the pleasure grounds beneath.

A thrill of remembrance came upon her. Surely she had trodden these trim-kept walks before, and inhaled the strange rich odour of the blossoming orange that hung heavy on the air?

Stopping, bewildered, she raised her hand to her brow. As she thus stood rapt in thought, the noise of approaching voices apprised her that Antiphates, leaning on the arm of Domenichino, drew near. Swift as lightning, recollection flashed across her. While the impatient monarch came towards her, guided by his servant, she half expected to see and hear the tiny elves who in her forest dreams had swung and sung their eerie refrain amid just such scenes as these.

M 2

When the King learned that she had not yet broken her fast, he commanded food to be brought to an arbour near at hand, where he himself joined his guest. He found much entertainment in trying to follow the movements of the little dog, who, summoned by his mistress, went through all his pretty tricks.

With unwonted softness in his voice and manner, Antiphates strove to set Fidunia at her ease, and to engage her in conversation. He led her on to speak of herself and of her previous lonely life. He encouraged her to tell him all that had befallen her since she left the forest.

Domenichino oftentimes listened in surprise. His master, hitherto so hasty and imperious, with rare patience, endeavoured to overcome Fidunia's timidity and reserve. Antiphates even forgot to murmur continually at his own affliction—nay, he felt a certain pleasure in claiming the young girl's assistance, as they wandered together in the gardens, or moved from room to room of the palace.

Day after day glided swiftly away, and life became a fresh pleasure to the weary King as he listened to the strange adventures and artless sayings of the ingenuous maiden. He derived perpetual amusement from her novel descriptions of familiar objects presented to him under a widely different aspect by her humorous remarks.

For years upon years he had existed with all of visible beauty veiled from his sight; and he now conjured up to himself an exquisite ideal of his youthful companion. Her low melodious voice, her gentle touch, and her soft light step, full of grace, taught him insensibly to dream of a far fairer form than poor Fidunia actually possessed.

He became so deeply interested in his new friend, that ere long that interest was merged in love. Morning, noon, and night, he was her inseparable companion, nor could he rest quiet when she was absent from him. He found in her society a nameless charm that tamed and softened his arrogant spirit. With extraordinary humility he learnt to defer to her slightest wish. With unwonted self-abnegation, he laid siege to the citadel of her heart.

Listening entranced to his tender words, there now ensued a period when, for the first time to the guileless Fidunia, if not to her more experienced suitor,

" Love took up the glass of Time, and turned it in his glowing hands ;
Every moment, lightly shaken, ran itself in golden sands.
Love took up the harp of Life, and smote on all the chords with might ;
Smote the chord of self, that, trembling, passed in music out of sight."

Antiphates soon told the wondering maiden all he had heard in the cave. His thoughts turned continually upon the mysterious prophecy, and they often held sweet counsel together over those singular but well-remembered words.

A dim foreboding of evil in the future, and an intense clinging to the peaceful joyous life of the present, led Fidunia to approach this subject with secret reluctance. An inward voice told her she possessed not beauty's potent charm ; yet she felt that to her blind monarch she was all in all. Again and again she had to stifle the rising fear of possible change in his love, and chided herself for unworthy thoughts and lukewarm energy.

With all the eagerness of his impetuous nature, Antiphates constantly recurred to the charge, urging Fidunia to do her utmost to deliver him from his infirmity. In glowing terms he depicted the pleasures of their common existence if he were able, not merely to hear and to feel, but to watch and to guide his heart's beloved through her future life.

As he spoke, the forest maid often felt the hidden talisman rise and fall with the heavings of her tender bosom. Obedient to the donor, she never disclosed its existence, even to Antiphates, or told him of her strange dreams. It needed, however, no small resolution on her part to avail herself of the charm so solemnly committed to her charge by Dame Anna. At length, unable longer to resist the oft-repeated solicitations of her royal lover, she faithfully promised him to exert her feeble powers to the utmost on his behalf.

With a lingering footstep she sought her chamber that evening, filled with awe at the prospect of invoking the aid of her scarce known friend. When all was silent for the night, Fidunia trimmed the classic lamp by her bedside, for it was the new moon, and no light came from without. Watched only by the wakeful Fido, she drew the sparkling prism from its accustomed place. Remembering her instructions, she placed it in the palm of her hand, then bent (for another's sake), on peering into futurity, she resolutely fixed her eyes on the talisman. Swaying to and fro with the intensity of her emotions, she chanted the required invocation:

> Strange gem, upon thy crystal core
> I gaze, the while I aid implore;
> Trembling upon the verge of fate,
> Oh, point my path ere yet too late!
> I fain would gain the boon I ask.
> Is mine the strength for such a task?
> Canst thou unloose the links that bind,
> Or vanquish powerful foes combined?
> Then show whate'er there lurks of art
> Within thine own mysterious heart;
> On thee I turn a hopeful eye,
> Bright stone of silence, make reply.

The magic stone grew larger and larger. Its

brilliant centre, like a searching eye, returned
Fidunia's gaze with dazzling refulgence. Heavier
and heavier drooped her falling lids, her recum-
bent form sought more and more the support of
her little couch, at length borne down by resistless force, she lay unnerved and motionless.

The lamp became extinguished. All was dark,
silent, and blank. Her corporeal frame slumbered
inert and passive. But now every spiritual faculty
throbbed into keen activity. The whole chamber
was filled with soft penetrating light. The kind
Anna's well-remembered form stood beside her.
With one hand she raised Fidunia on her couch,
with the other she pointed towards the south.

To Fidunia's intense surprise, she beheld a ray
of moonlight illumine the sombre waters of the Bay
of Deva, reaching in one narrow unbroken line to
what she well knew as the distant though hitherto
unvisited island of Spera. She gazed bewildered
from her raised alcove, which commanded an easy
view of the landscape beneath, through the wide,
open windows.

How could the small silver horn of the newborn
moon cast such brilliant light on the dark ocean?
She turned a troubled glance towards her unwonted
visitant, but her voice was spell-bound; the questions
she fain would have uttered died upon her lips.

With a sad and solemn gesture her protectress still pointed towards the heights of Spera, then sighed, rather than said these lines :

> Far, far o'er the depths of that shimm'ring blue sea,
> The drops trickle slowly so sought for by thee;
> Enwrapt by the jealous embrace of the deep,
> A lake without sky, without motion doth sleep.
> Though distant, and hidden the shrine of the cave
> By the busy bright waters its entrance that lave,
> Yet only the touch of an innocent maiden
> Can e'er give effect to those drops virtue-laden.
> At midnight a ray shall illumine the portal
> All sombre and silent, ne'er threaded by mortal.
> At midnight, by moonlight, that path can be crossed,
> By her, who heroic, ne'er counteth the cost.
> Oh, chilly the ocean, and lonely the hour,
> Or the charm that thou seekest is reft of its power ;
> And voiceless and mute thine endeavours must be,
> Or fruitless thy labours and harmful to thee.
> Yet, maiden, forbear ! ere thou challenge the spell ·
> Remember—with thee and with thine it is well !
> In thee and thy love the blind monarch is blest :
> Then dwell in his palace—Fidunia—at rest.

As the last couplet fell on Fidunia's ears all else became as nought. The dear thought of her first and faithful lover filled her imaginative mind. What recked she of trouble or sorrow to be undergone in his service! Would she not even give life itself for the sake of him who had first called into existence all the passionate but unknown wealth of her unselfish soul! Dreamily she recalled to her self his whispered vows, his ardent tones, and thus from waking dreams slowly fell on sleep, undisturbed and profound.

It was late the following morning before she awoke to the realities of life. As she dressed herself she pondered much over the visions of the night. Was all a dream, like her forest fancies ?

She looked everywhere for the talisman, but it was nowhere to be seen. Its absence weighed somewhat heavily on her mind. The reality of her midnight experience was brought home to her, as she perpetually missed the shining stone from its wonted hiding-place.

Fidunia now hastened to her monarch's presence. Considering that the loss of the talisman released her from her promise of secrecy, she confided its whole history to the astonished King. She told him also her waking vision of the previous night. She described Dame Anna's appearance, and repeated some of her words.

Thoroughly roused Antiphates entreated Fidunia to keep nothing more concealed from him. Using all his powers of persuasion he at length drew from her unwilling lips the particulars of her three wild forest dreams.

In a voice trembling with emotion he hailed the

FIDO AND FIDUNIA.

"Thoroughly roused, Antiphates entreated Fidunia to keep nothing more concealed
from him "—P. 17c.

forest maiden as his predestined deliverer, nor was his eager curiosity satisfied till he had asked innumerable questions. Fidunia sighed as she noted his feverish agitation. Remembering the warning contained in the last rhythmical lines, she feared lest his hopes should be dashed to the ground.

As they sat together in his favourite turret above the castle porch, he explained to her that rumour spoke of a hidden cave in the Isle of Spera. Recalling to mind the line of light she had so distinctly seen across the bay, Fidunia pointed it out as having terminated beneath the highest peak of the island. Antiphates decided that an endeavour to find the cave should be made when the moon next became full. He would fain himself have aided in the search; but Fidunia, anxious to have her mind steadfastly set on the one object of the expedition, persuaded him to remain within the palace, and to allow her to go forth guarded only by Domenichino.

Domenichino secretly hired, as for his own use, one of the boats belonging to a fisherman of Spera. He carefully questioned the men of the place about their island. They all seemed aware of the probable existence of a cave only accessible from the sea, but partly from the dreamy indolence common to those climes, partly from superstition, no one had as yet discovered its entrance. A thousand old legends,

however, sung of the hidden beauties of this wondrous grotto, a hundred wild tales were told among
these simple people of the magic and wonder-working
fountain therein concealed from mortal eyes.

At last the time arrived when, at midnight,
Cynthia should reach her cold meridian of beauty.
Fidunia resolved to leave Fido for the first time behind her. She committed him to the willing charge
of the King, but the little animal, who from the first
had taken a dislike to Antiphates, could not be got
away from his mistress's chamber. There, extended
on the moonlit verandah, he remained during her
absence, disconsolate and wakeful.

It was a night of peaceful calm. As the sturdy
rowers urged on their vessel, her bows parted the
waters into a thousand phosphorescent ripples, which,
widening as the boat moved onward, spread into one
broad, flaming wake in their rear.

Fidunia carried with her an ancient gold goblet,
wherein the King besought her to place the precious
drops, should she succeed in obtaining them. Grasp-
ing it tightly in her hand, as if to persuade herself
she was not dreaming, she gazed awestruck on the
overwhelming beauty of the landscape, arrayed in
night's fairest covering.

Already distant, the City of Deva lay white and
ghost-like under the moon's pale ray. Here and

there a gleam of light showed that there were watchers on land, and from the high turret window of Castle Xylina one ruddy gleam shot a quivering reflection far along the ever-lengthening track of their little craft.

Before them the nearing crags of Spera rose abrupt and beetling towards the sky. The boat moved rapidly along. Now became audible the surging swell and low muffled boom of the ocean, ever chafing, ever restless, even when apparently at peace ; and ever repelled by those giant sentinels of the deep. Numbers of sea-birds, disturbed by the unwonted splash of oars, wheeled screaming above their heads, and suddenly brought to Fidunia's mind with agitating distinctness the recollection of her second forest dream.

But all other thoughts were merged in the approaching performance of her self-imposed task. They had gradually rounded the opening to a little bay where the water seemed more shallow, and the sea only broke in tiny wavelets upon a small shelf of pearly white sand. Here Fidunia stepped from the boat. Leaving human companionship behind, she slowly paced along the narrow margin. Finally, following the moon-lit line and heedful of Domenichino's oft-repeated instructions, she disappeared behind the frowning ledge of rock which bounded the narrow inlet.

Only a very few minutes after she had thus gone from their sight, they could hear dimly across the intervening waters, the faint tolling of the midnight bells in the great City. In indescribable anxiety Domenichino, who alone (among these rude boat-men) knew her peril, counted the minutes till Fidunia's return, and resolved that at the expiration of a certain time he would at all risks persist in following the unprotected maiden.

But, ere the appointed period had elapsed, Fidunia, with buoyant steps, turned swiftly the dark boundary and rapidly drew near. High resolve sat upon her brow and stamped her features with a noble ardour. Closely clasped to her bosom she held the precious vase, but to no mortal ear might she unfold the thrilling tale of her solitary experience.

Had she within those mystic precincts heard a warning voice which bade her pause ere she dashed the cup of earthly happiness from her lips? How and where had she obtained the crystal liquid that leapt and sparkled in its golden prison? Had she entered the ice-cold waters and braved the wave-engulfing arms of the merry, malicious mer-men, who warily watch, and at the midnight hour have power to bear to their coral haunts the bold earth-maiden who shall step within their native element?

These, and numberless other questions, crowded

into Domenichino's mind as he sped to meet her; but she raised her finger to her lips, and with a mute gesture of entreaty silently took her place in the little vessel. The weather-beaten boatmen shrank back as she passed them by, her hair and garments glistening with a thousand rainbow-coloured drops; yet, as she dreamily took her place in the stern, one, less bashful than his compeers, awkwardly placed his rough coat so as to shelter and keep her warm.

The wind had arisen. It swept moaningly around, hurrying dark clouds across the face of the moon, and presently shrouding her altogether from their sight. But the red tower-light from distant Xylina guided the homeward-bound crew, and ere very long they were safely landed below the slumbéring City.

Still voiceless, Fidunia, with lagging footsteps, ascended the steep hill. Her energy was gone; she leant heavily on Domenichino's arm, and but for his aid must have fallen more than once exhausted by the way. At last the castle was reached. In answer to her signal the faithful esquire knocked at his master's turret door. An impatient voice bade them enter. Antiphates himself, stumbling hastily to meet them, started as he took Fidunia's cold hand in his. She gently withstood his eager inquiries and solicitude for her health. " Sire," she murmured, "I am

very weary, but these poor hands must this night
bathe your eyes."

At her words the King, obedient, sank on a couch
near at hand, and Fidunia, dipping her fingers into
the golden goblet, timidly pressed them again and
again over his burning eyelids. Her cool, soft touch
soothed his irritated nerves and brought refreshing
peace to his restless mind. A strange calm folded
its enshadowing wings around those busy brows
and wrapt the imperious monarch in a sweet and
childlike slumber.

Raising her finger again to her lips, in token of
silence, and signing to Domenichino to leave his
sovereign for the night, Fidunia quitted the turret
chamber and sought her own apartment. Here the
listening Fido greeted her approaching footsteps with
a whine of delight, and testified his joy at her return
by many expressive gambols.

Long into the night she sat on her balcony, acting
over in thought again and again the exciting scenes
of that eventful evening. It seemed to her she had
only just fallen asleep when she was suddenly startled
from her slumbers by a loud pæan of rejoicing blown
from the castle wall by the silver trumpets.

For a moment recollection failed her, but then glad
certainty flashed on her mind, and, as if to make
assurance doubly sure, some of the women of the

palace, rushing abruptly into her chamber, confirmed the glad tidings. They urged her to arise and dress in haste, for the King could not rest till he had seen and thanked his deliverer in person.

Fidunia hurriedly arrayed herself. Accompanied by Fido, she hastened along the now well-known passages of the palace. She ascended the broad stairs and passed the tall guards in the corridor, with their nodding plumes. The doors of the presence chamber were thrown open before her. On the threshold she stood a moment irresolute. Then, notwithstanding their intimacy, knowing his newly-gained power, she advanced timidly towards the great King. There was a pause, she raised her eyes to his. The monarch seemed transformed! Instead of half-closed, unseeing eyes, and all the accompanying hesitation and uncertainty, two searching orbs now bent their dark majesty full on the bashful maiden. In that one moment she drank in the fatal secret, which no after-words could disguise.

It was but too true!

A passionate adorer of beauty, Antiphates had, during the past months, almost unknown to himself, clothed his unseen love with perfect loveliness. His heart therefore beat high with expectation as her footfall was heard at the door, and when, with her

N

attendant Fido, she entered alone, he could not control the impulse of disappointment too plainly written on his expressive, speaking countenance.

The dawn of light on his long-darkened orbs revealed to him the unattractive colouring and irregular features of the being he had in blindness learned to adore, and no self-command on his part could conceal from love's unerring instinct his change of mood.

Now, however, with well-simulated alacrity, he rose from his throne. Stepping down with a free, unfettered gait, widely different from his wonted stumbling manner, he took the maiden's hand in his own. Pouring confused and hurried thanks into her ear, he led her to the seat where she had passed so many happy hours.

In vain he strove to conjure back the fascination Fidunia once possessed for him. Oh! subtle influence! who can accurately define the thrilling tie that makes the one we love different from all the world beside? who, when the frail chain of enchantment is once severed, can join again those mystic links?

The King and Fidunia conversed in low tones, apparently unchanged: the gay courtiers around at least observed no cloud on the horizon. Waiting within call, they clustered eagerly around Domenichino to hear his adventures of the previous night, and to discuss together the approaching marriage of the maiden, now beloved by all, with their fortune-favoured prince. They recked not of the cold shadow that crept slowly into the little maid's heart, and clouded her fair and hitherto untroubled sky.

Fido alone, close and vigilant, marked the awakening sorrow of his beloved mistress. He felt the hand that caressed him grow cold and pulseless. He noted the accent of despair in Fidunia's choking voice. His unsophisticated nature rose indignant at the selfishness of the human friend, who (after such vows breathed, and responded to by her to whom they were addressed), could change and grow indifferent to the being who had gone through so much for his sake.

How true it is that maidens, like flowers, expand in the presence of him they love, in the warm sunshine of adoration. When that cheering beam is withdrawn, how colourless and scentless, how devoid of beauty, do their drooping blossoms become !

Even so it was with Fidunia, the happy light that had of late dawned in her gray eyes now faded away. Hour after hour she wept alone on her sleepless pillow, sadly musing over times departed,

" Departed never to return."

N 2

One wakeful night she poured out her thoughts in
these words:

The silent hour of night prevailed, the Earth
Was in her first and dewy slumber, while
The Moon unveiled her pure and peerless light,
And threw her radiance o'er the dusky haunts
Of men.
          An atom on the world's broad breast
Alone, beneath those chilly beams I mused,
On Death and Immortality.
                    My soul
Sped swiftly upward on the ethereal ray,
And left enthralled the grosser part of self,
The slumbering mortal portion of my frame.

    *   *   *   *   *

The spirit world was gained, and for a space
Enchantment wove mine aching heart a strange
Bright web of many hued delight. She gave
To that brief Dream all the reality
That made its flying moments passing sweet.
The kindly echoes lent their magic aid,
And tones reverberated in mine ear
Whose music gently whispered rapture, not
Of Earth, but of some far-off lovely Land,
A Time when all that is not yet may be.

    *   *   *   *   *

With trembling sigh, from happiness too great,
I all unknowing broke the mystic spell,
And shivering back, through dark and dreary ways,
No Moon to guide the weary feet, no Light
To cheer the falling spirit, once again
Within dull clay poor Psyche found her home,
And woke to bitter loneliness and woe.

She had in truth a rough awakening from her dream of happiness. As day by day the restless monarch showed more and more the change in his feelings that perfect vision had wrought, Fidunia not only passed through the deep waters of sorrow in realizing his alienation, but experienced moreover a fresh and equally poignant pain as the veil of illusion fell from her disenchanted eyes, and taught the simple-hearted young girl that she could 'never again regard her monarch with the same trusting faith.

To one of hasty impulsive temperament like Antiphates, dissimulation proved impossible : however much he was bound, alike by the ties of honour and of gratitude, to keep the vows publicly pledged to his deliverer, he could not forgive the hapless girl her lack of outward beauty. He valued not the delicate refinement of her nature. He marked not the ethereal spirit that shone unconquerable through her transparent eye. His affection had been of the earth, earthy ; evanescent as frail mortality itself.

Nor was Fidunia's spirit formed in a mould to sicken and die of unrequited affection. In happier days, the happiest of her short life, she had, in spite of the vast difference in their ages, learned to regard the gifted King with something akin to reverential love. The eager wooing of one so talented and fascinating could not fail to produce some corresponding

effect on the imagination of the forest maiden. Not
unsolicited she had yielded up her gentle heart, and
come gradually to centre all the hopes and thoughts
of her young life upon Antiphates.

She now grew to spend longer hours each day in
wandering round the precincts of Xylina. The child
of nature, she ever found her truest solace beneath
the wide canopy of heaven. There no walls pent in
her labouring sobs, no human eye beheld the slowly
falling tears, mourners over a vanished past, that
welled up one by one from her burning heart ; tears
that slowly rising, purified still further her much
afflicted spirit, and weaned her soul from the earthly
love which for a time had satisfied that strange immortal portion of mortality.

Fido, ever beside his mistress, grew like her, pen-
sive and forlorn. He knew she was in grief, and
his mute sympathy gave her comfort, as together they
climbed through the mazy wood, or explored the
hills that rose behind the castle.

In these wanderings, Fidunia came frequently to a
knoll, commanding the lovely expanse of waters
beneath. Looking across the broad bay of Deva, the
horizon was bounded only by the fair island of Spera,
so fraught with memory's brightest records. Here
upon a bank of wild thyme, sheltered by the cool
olive trees, and fanned by the passing breeze, she

pondered over her mysterious lot, and shudderingly thought of the blank untrodden future.·

But counsel and comfort already approached. One day as she thus sat, rapt and musing, a gentle voice addressed her; turning half alarmed, she beheld the sweetest face her eyes had ever dwelt upon. That countenance shone with heaven-born beauty. " Sister Angela " (for thus the stranger was called) had also sorrowed, but she had found lasting comfort in the convent of Saint Sebastian. This monastery was near at hand, though partially concealed by the dense foliage and the masses of creepers which clothed its outer walls. Angela had oftentimes seen and yearned over the sorrowful young girl, and at last, issuing forth, ventured to greet her.

She tenderly saluted Fidunia, who, before long, learnt to love and trust her new friend. She soon came daily to seek for guidance and comfort at her hands, confiding to Angela's sympathizing ears the chequered story of her brief life.

Meantime, to add still further to the griefs of poor Fidunia, her little dog disappeared. She first missed him one afternoon as, after long converse with her new found friend, she turned to descend the grassy slopes to Castle Xylina.

During those hours she had formed a high and holy resolution. Alone in the world, she aspired to

become one of the sisterhood to whom Angela be-
longed, and to find an asylum for her wearied
wounded heart within the sacred walls of Saint
Sebastian.

On reaching the Castle, Fidunia sought everywhere
for Fido, but no one had seen him, or could tell
whither he had gone. While occupied in threading
the long passages and calling anxiously for her
missing companion, she met Domenichino hastening
to entreat her attendance on the King. Without
returning to her chamber to alter her attire, Fidunia
turned and accompanied him to the royal presence.

Antiphates met her at the entrance of the hall.
In kind yet constrained tones the monarch condoled
with her as he heard of Fido's disappearance. He
gave orders moreover that the strictest search should
at once be instituted throughout Deva and its environs for Fidunia's dear little favourite.

"But now," continued the King, leading her to a
deep embrasure, whence could be seen the fair landscape beneath, "I am anxious you should name the
day for the ceremony that is to unite the debtor to
his mistress, and thus permit me to fulfil my plighted
troth." So saying, he carried her hand lightly to his
lips, and looked searchingly upon her. But even his
bold eyes fell rebuked beneath Fidunia's pure enquir-
ing gaze, now divested of all hesitation or embarrass-

ment. No word of reproach for his altered behaviour towards her, since she had restored his sight, fell from her. No murmur escaped her. But her voice quavered as, in a few simple sentences, she unfolded to him the purpose she had that day formed of taking upon herself the vows of Saint Sebastian.

A sense of momentary shame at his own want of generosity dyed the King's rough cheek a deeper hue. He felt his inability to urge Fidunia with any zest to renounce her lofty aspirations. He strove to conceal his satisfaction, but he knew too well that her voluntary self-devotion relieved him from a perplexing dilemma.

Nevertheless he cast about in his mind for some form of remonstrance ; but before he could frame the words on his unwilling lips, she was gone.

Stung to her inmost heart by the inscrutable changes in his variable nature, and already overwrought by the day's emotions, the hapless Fidunia only reached her chamber in time to shut from every human eye her deadly struggle, her last overwhelming battle with wounded mortal love.

Days slowly elapsed without intelligence of Fido, and the arrangements became gradually completed by which, upon the Festival of All Saints, Fidunia was to enter her noviciate.

All Hallow's Eve drew near. On the morrow the

lonely Fidunia was to bid farewell to the outer
world, and rest her wearied tempest-tossed head
within the peaceful cloistered shades.

She sought her luxurious chamber for the last time,
and unfastening the window, stepped out on the
broad balcony. The glorious full moon once more
illuminated with clear cold light each beloved object
in the exquisite panorama so dear to her.

Human sorrow asserted its own in the maiden's
breast, as in spirit she bade farewell to the slumbering
monarch who, for a brief period, had been her sun and
firmament, the "all" for which in the forest depths
her innocent soul had insensibly pined.

A sudden pattering footstep sounded near, and
looking inwards, lo! through the moonlit chamber,
approached the truant Fido. In the imperfect light
he seemed faint and weary; but Fidunia sprang to
meet him, and raised and fondled the little wanderer in her arms, asking him the while many a
question about his strange absence, half reproaching
him for his desertion.

As she held the little dog close to her breast,
rejoicing over his return, she felt something of a
novel character around his neck. She gently un-
fastened a cord, and found attached to it a small
phial carefully sealed, yet emitting a wondrous
fragrance.

Somehow assuming from her companion's quiescent attitude that the flask was for her own use, she slipped it into her bosom, and forgetting all else, again yielded herself to vague yearnings over the unfulfilled visions of the past. It was long before she stepped from the window, and placing Fido on the ground prepared for her last night's rest in the palace.

As she let down the now lengthened tresses of her thick hair, Fido though evidently exhausted, refused to lie down. Seemingly ill at ease, he watched her every movement with painful anxiety. When at length she drew near the marble bath, wherein she nightly plunged, his agitation knew no bounds, and as in undressing she displaced the phial from her garments he uttered a series of short sharp barks restlessly springing the while backwards and forwards from his mistress to the edge of the alcove. So close was the companionship between Fidunia and her faithful companion, that she at once divined his meaning, and undoing the seal and extracting the stopper from the bottle, she emptied its contents into the water. Scarcely had she done so when the whole chamber became filled with a delicious perfume. As one in a trance, half overcome by the powerful scent, Fidunia entered her bath, and felt at once the extraordinary invigorating power which seemed to emanate from those few drops of liquid.

All sorrow was lifted from her heart. Already in imagination she joined in the sweet praiseful strains of the Sebastian sisters. Angelic forms moved around her, and the moon's pale rays at length guided the weary maiden to her pillow. Stretching out one soft arm over her faithful dog, lying in his cot by her side, and lulled by a foretaste of heaven's own music, Fidunia sank into dreams of ecstatic beauty.

The loud pealing of a thousand bells for the Festival of All Saints at last awoke the neophyte from her deep repose. For a moment she started and half forgot her resting place; but her eye fell upon her little dog. Something strange in his attitude struck her. Startled, she sprang to her feet and bent over him.

His sleep was surely very deep! Yes, Fidunia! sound are those slumbers from which not even the touch of thy beloved hand can rouse his wearied form, or call forth a response from the wistful eyes, wont to hang upon thy lightest gesture.

With an exceeding bitter cry, Fidunia fell beside her lost favourite and vainly chafed his stiffening limbs. As she stooped over him, her eyes swimming in tears, she perceived in the morning light a small scroll lying on the floor by his couch. She hastily raised it, and noted "This for Fidunia" traced upon the outer covering. She tore it open, and through the mists of sorrow that perpetually dimmed her vision, she read these words :

"Sweet daughter, when thou readest this, thy faithful servant will be no more. Know that the little dog, Fido, through many past days and nights hath mourned over thine exceeding sorrow and thy low estate.

"He held thee altogether lovely, but he knew from human fellowship that those who owed most to thy labours, my child, had weighed thine outward beauty in the balance and found it wanting. He watched thine affliction till his own heart went nigh to break ; and then, calling to remembrance my counsels and assistance to thee, he left thy side, and through many hardships and with great fatigue he gained once more my little cottage by the wide and spreading common. I made known to him that the gift of earthly beauty could only be thine through the self-sacrifice of one who loved thee to the death. Thy faithful companion hath cheerfully laid down his sinless existence for thy dear sake.

"Heaven guard thee and guide thee, Fidunia !

"ANNA."

As Fidunia, penetrated to her very inmost soul by the dying fidelity of her beloved dog, sank again over his inanimate frame, a loud and persistent knocking made itself heard at her chamber door. She had barely time to cast on her outer garments before the palace women, alarmed by her first cry, and hearing no response to their summons, thrust open the door and drew inquisitively near the weeping maiden.

Fidunia rose from her knees, and casting an indignant look on the amazed intruders, she exclaimed, " Behold your thoughtless work ! It was through you and yours that my poor dog learnt the small esteem in which his mistress was held, and has thus been goaded to his death."

No answer came from the gathering throng. Awed and abashed, they herded together. Whence came the ineffable beauty that sat upon Fidunia's brow, and cast a radiance over her shining hair ? That it was the forest maiden none could doubt, but how exquisitely soft and fair her lineaments, as standing in the morning sun before her dead comrade's couch, she gave vent to her feelings of passionate reproach.

At this moment Domenichino, hastily entering, heralded the King's approach. The news of the death of Fido and of Fidunia's miraculous and newborn beauty had spread like wild-fire through the Castle.

Antiphates, no less bewildered than his subjects,

hesitated half awe-struck on the threshold of
the young girl's chamber, which he now for the
first time proposed to enter. Recovering himself
promptly, however, with an imperious gesture he
signed to his surrounding people to leave the apartment, and then slowly advanced to the now silent but
still weeping Fidunia.

In bygone days, all unknown to the sightless
monarch, the very sound of his approaching footsteps
had power to suffuse her cheek with blushes. Now
coldly conscious of his presence, she stood before
him without responsive sign, the loveliest creature
upon God's wide earth, the realized ideal of his
fairest dreams.

Wrapped in her white morning robe, with her yet
unbound hair falling back in rich clustering masses
from her pure pale brow and pearly skin of dazzling
whiteness; a solemn depth shone from her dark
blue eyes, bearing still a wealth of tears unshed ;
while a faint evanescent colour like the transparent
petal of the wood anemone played upon her rounded
cheek.

All unknown to herself, clothed in this wondrous
panoply of beauty, Fidunia awaited her sovereign's
commands. To her unspeakable surprise the monarch seemed overcome with some unbidden emotion.
Again and again he vainly assayed to speak ; at

length, drawing near, he bent his proud knee before her, and in agitated tones besought her pardon.

"Sire," replied Fidunia, "as regards myself, I have little to forgive, but would that my dumb companion had been spared the knowledge that hath cost him his faithful life."

"Oh, Fidunia!" cried the enamoured Prince, "forget these sad weeks wherein we have suffered disquiet, and during which untoward shadows have obscured my vision, and consent, as you once promised, to be my bride. I swear to you, my darling," continued he, pressing closer to the shrinking girl, "that in my love and tender care you shall find consolation even for the death of your poor lost favourite."

With an effort Fidunia extricated her hand from his nervous grasp, and the red flush of indignation mounting higher and higher, she exclaimed, "Nay, my liege, this is neither the time nor the place wherein to renew the vows which of late have sat so light on thy heart and conscience. Here in the presence of the faithful dead, spare me, I pray thee, all reference to the unfaithful past. That chapter is closed for ever. On this morning, with thy free consent, I take upon myself new and holy vows. Yes," repeated she, raising her speaking eyes to the glorious eastern sky, "I am accounted worthy to become the lowly bride of Heaven." And as if in confirmation of her words, a gust of wind brought faintly to their ears, through the wide open window, the glad chiming of the Saint Sebastian bells, ringing in anticipation of the ceremonial of the day.

"Now by my crown and kingdom," whispered Antiphates, in burning ardent tones, "that thou never shalt become, for mine thou art and mine thou shalt remain while I have life and power to keep thee." So saying he sprang to his feet and enfolding Fidunia in his arms, pressed her fiercely to his breast.

Weary and distraught, and well nigh overcome with the struggle, as she felt the loud pulsations of his throbbing heart, and experienced the mesmeric influence of strong earthly passion, the sorely bestead maiden breathed from her fainting soul an earnest prayer for guidance; and her silent petition for aid in the hour of need was answered.

A low strain of music sounded through the chamber, and the reluctant King involuntarily released his trembling captive, as the door slowly opening admitted two by two the veiled and white arrayed sisters of Saint Sebastian coming to adorn their promised novice for the approaching ceremony.

In vain the distracted Prince commanded them to pause in their holy duties, in vain he implored Fidunia to delay even for a day her irrevocable vows.

Borne back by the gentle but resistless force of

the sacred band, and secretly abashed at the recollection of his own conduct, Antiphates stood spell-
bound, devouring with hungry eyes the peerless
beauty of the maid, whom too late, he knew to be
the one golden hope of his life. They arrayed her
in bridal robes of exceeding splendour. They placed
a coronal of blooming orange flowers upon her fault-
less head.

When all was completed Fidunia, turning to Domenichino, pleaded with him to convey what remained of her devoted servant to the little thymy
knoll beneath the olive trees, and there within easy
reach of her convent walls, to lay to rest the still
beautiful form of the faithful Fido.

Then, stepping aside as if to bid him farewell,
she raised and kissed the silent Prince's hand, murmuring in tones that he alone could hear, "while
life lasts I shall pray for thee." Ere he could re-
spond the procession slowly re-formed, and descending
the broad palace-stairs, swept onwards along the
avenue of grassy sward, and through the orange-
scented gardens of Xylina to the hallowed precincts
of Saint Sebastian on the Hill.

Within the chapel where the holy fathers waited,
many had collected to witness the ceremony, but
the King and his cortége occupied the places nearest
to the sisters and the young aspirant.

Through his intervention her meditations were yet again disturbed, as he besought her once more to turn from her purpose, and to remain amid the outer world as his loved and honoured bride. She steadfastly refused to listen to his entreaties. The service proceeded, and the novice at length prepared to pass through the iron gateway that should now close to all eternity between her and the world without. A ray from heaven fell on her beautiful figure, and illumined her devout features, as she stood waiting to receive the white consecrated veil of the sisterhood.

The long enveloping folds shrouded her from head to foot, and as Fidunia's golden head disappeared for ever from the sight of man, the whole air became filled with the celestial voices of the choir, singing these glorious words,

"She is not dead, but liveth."

EUDÆMON:

OR

THE ENCHANTER OF THE NORTH.

EUDÆMON.   P. 199.

EUDÆMON :

OR

THE ENCHANTER OF THE NORTH.

On the eastern side of the Isle of Raasay there still stands a lonely ruin known as Castle Brochel. Perched upon precipitous rocks at the very verge of the ocean, it is easy to imagine how, armed and provisioned, this fortress held its own amid the perpetual warfare of early Celtic times.

Castle Brochel has always borne a doubtful reputation. According to tradition, it was originally built with the price of blood, for the ancient legend runs somewhat after this fashion.

Shiel Torquil went forth with his dogs one morning to hunt the red deer on the wild mountains Blaven and Glamaig, in the neighbouring Island of Skye. Shiel Torquil had with him only one retainer, but he was a host in himself, being surnamed, from his immense size and strength, the Gillie More. After some time they sighted a stag. In the ardour of the chase the dogs soon ran out of sight, pursuing their quarry towards the shore at Sligachan.

Now it so happened that the young Kreshinish in his galley was anchored on that side of the island within sight of the beach. He saw the hunted animal about to take to the water, and swim, as deer are often known to do, across the narrow strait which lies between Skye and Raasay. Kreshinish and his men at once landed and took possession, not only of the stag itself, but of the dogs which, panting and exhausted, were unable to offer any resistance.

Shiel Torquil presently appeared on the scene and angrily asked for his deer and his hounds. Kreshinish refused to deliver them up. A bloody struggle ensued, during which the Gillie More inflicted a fatal wound upon the ill-fated young chieftain who unwittingly (at first) had interfered with the sports of another. This brought the affray to a speedy conclusion, and Shiel Torquil with his follower carried off deer and dogs in triumph.

Not long after this the poor old father of Kreshinish came to Skye to seek for the murderer of his son, and publicly offered the reward of a bag of silver to any one who would show him the guilty man. The Gillie More, hearing of the promised guerdon, boldly entered the presence of the elder Kreshinish. Con-

fessing that he himself had slain the youthful chieftain, he urged in self-defence the young man's over-
bearing conduct in attempting to carry off Shiel
Torquil's stag-hounds and game.

The bereaved father, obliged by the stringent laws
of Highland honour to fulfil his solemn promise, reluctantly bestowed the bag of silver on the very man
who had cut off his only child in the early bloom of
manhood. The Gillie More, however, haunted by
remorse, and still fearing the avenger's footstep,
entreated his master to accept the money and build
therewith a retreat for them both.

Shiel Torquil granted his henchman's request.
After some time spent in searching for a suitable
site, they at last selected the wild easterly shore
of Raasay. Here were speedily raised the frowning
walls of Castle Brochel. Secured from sudden attack
by the inaccessible situation of their refuge, the
Gillie More and his master lived in peace for
many years.

Their retired habits, and their dislike to intruders,
coupled with this strange tale of robbery and mur-
der, caused the Castle, though newly-built, to be
regarded with no friendly eye. When they died, it
was left untenanted for a considerable time. Many
reports were circulated concerning the strange sights
and sounds to be seen and heard at the eerie hour of

twilight, or amid the silent watches of the night, by the belated traveller who chanced to pass that way by sea or by land.

At the period of which we speak, Castle Brochel had however for some time been inhabited by a being whose origin was partially shrouded in mystery, the gloomy Eudæmon, known as the "Enchanter of the North."

Long years ago, Valbiorn, the wild sea-king, persuaded the lovely Bragela, Sorglan's fair-haired daughter, to fly with him from her home. Terrible was Sorglan's wrath when he discovered that his hereditary enemy had deprived him of his only child, and undying was his resentment. But filial disobedience brought its own punishment. Before very long the restless Valbiorn was once more roaming alone on the high seas, spreading war and confusion in his wake.

It was next rumoured that the gentle Bragela, heart-broken and deserted, had, with her little babe and an old and faithful attendant, one-eyed Donald, taken up her abode in the lonely Castle Brochel. Here she reared her son, within whose infant mind the powers of good and evil seemed to struggle with unwonted energy.

Unceasing were the prayers that the loving mother offered up over her child, for his strange nature caused her many tears. At times he would sit contented by her side, and fixing on her · his large dark eyes, listen attentively to her words of instruction and wisdom. Or wandering with her, as soon as he could run alone, over the hills near at hand, he learnt the names and properties of various medicinal herbs, and the hours when they should be gathered to render their use efficacious. Wondrously effectual was the healing touch he inherited from his fair young mother and ,brought to light in future years.

On other days a mad spirit of wild wantonness seemed to possess the boy. He would destroy everything upon which he could lay his hand, or tear along recklessly over the rugged walls and dangerous precipices on which the Castle stood, where a single false step would have dashed him to pieces on the rocks beneath. If his mother tearfully besought him to return to her, he would burst into loud fits of laughter, and shriek until the very sea-birds flew affrighted from the spot.

When these strange paroxysms seized him, Bragela found that nothing had the least effect upon her wayward child save music. It was wholly by accident she first discovered the soothing charm of melody on his turbulent nature.

One day, after watching his wild antics till her

very heart grew sick within her, she re-entered the hall wearied and discouraged. Gradually consoling herself as she remembered how often the young rebel had come down in safety from his perilous haunts, she drew to her the harp, her father's gift in days of yore, which in all her wanderings she had carried with her. Striking chord after chord on its well-worn strings, she at length began to mingle her sweet voice with its thrilling tones. She sang of her childhood's happy home, and her tenderly-loved father, of the still beloved though faithless Valbiorn, of the perils they had together undergone, of the blissful hours she had once enjoyed when the fierce warrior forgot everything save her gentle strains, and lay entranced at her feet drinking in every word, and whispering in ardent tones that "her voice was as that of the angels in heaven."

She would have sung on of sorrow and forlorn solitude, but voice and heart alike failed her. Clasping her arms around her cold harp, the forsaken Bragela bowed her head on its shoulder and wept aloud.

But a little rough hand was laid upon her neck. " Mother, mother," whispered her boy ; "you must not weep, you are not forlorn or lonely, for I am here to care for you, and to protect you."

Surprised and touched, Bragela turned to look upon the child. The wild light had died out of his eyes, and in its place shone through those brilliant orbs the tender protecting instinct of his sex. He drew closer to her, and pressing his little curly head on her soft bosom, he murmured, " I am sorry, mother dear ; forgive me this time."

Poor Bragela gladly folded the young truant to her heart. Henceforward she derived unspeakable comfort from this new influence over his boisterous spirit. For his sake she cheerfully resumed the art she had deemed laid aside for ever. When the wild fit again and again returned upon her boy, she would even carry her harp into the outer court. There inuring herself, with all a mother's courage, to behold without shuddering his maddest freaks, by her sweet singing and playing she gradually lured him to her side, and awakened his better self.

These happy days, however, could not continue for ever. Eudæmon's mother had gone through too many trials, and was of too tender a nature to endure such grief with impunity. There came a time when the gentle Bragela laid down her wearied head to rest ; her dim eye kindled not with affection when her terrified boy bent over her, her cold hand for the first time gave him no responsive caress. Her sorrows were over, but loud and long were the lamentations of her child ; thus left alone with one poor old man and his faithful dog Luachan.

At dead of night strange lights and sounds arose about that rugged dwelling. Watchers at a distance beheld the lonely castle enveloped in fiery smoke. Amid the wreathing vapours a figure of unearthly pro- portions carried to the sea a white-robed form with long flowing hair. The repentant Valbiorn, too late to save, or even to hold converse with his neglected Bragela, bore to his immortal home her precious remains. There he was able by his magic skill to endow her inanimate body with the semblance of life. He mournfully placed the beautiful image in the vaulted halls of Thuisto, where he could for ever gaze on the fatal beauty that had brought such misfortune on its possessor.

Valbiorn tried every art to persuade his son to accompany him ; but before her death Bragela had warned her child of the cruel nature of the sea-kings. She told him of her humble trust that notwithstanding her early disobedience (so heartily repented of), her soul might ascend to heaven, and though the still heathen Valbiorn could take her body, yet she felt her spirit would be safe with Him who gave it.

She explained to Eudæmon that if he came under his dread father's influence, the sea-king and his wild companions would strive their utmost to make him forget and neglect her careful instructions. She entreated him to be steadfast in his resistance to temptation, prophesying that eventually he might even have the great happiness of rescuing his father from the darkness of heathendom; if only he lived on in faith and simplicity, serving his unseen but all-powerful Maker, studying the books she left him, and endeavouring as best he might to help the poor ignorant Highlanders around.

The crafty Valbiorn finding all his endeavours powerless to persuade Eudæmon to quit his abode of safety, resolved to destroy his disobedient son and his refuge at the same time. But here the loving mother's foresight helped in the preservation of her child. Among the other treasures carried by the fugitive Bragela to Castle Brochel, were some fowls of the famous breed first reared by the witch Fantunina, which by their watchfulness are able to protect their possessors from the powers of evil.

Night after night, therefore, when the emissaries of the baffled sea-king strove to destroy the Castle by fire, the magic cock, ever on the alert, flapped his wings and loudly proclaimed the approach of danger. Then Eudæmon arising from his lonely couch, wrestled in silent prayer until the first faint streaks of daylight in the eastern sky showed him that night's dominion was over. Thus baulked of his prey, Val-

biorn withdrew in a terrible tempest to Thuisto, nor
did his son again hear of him for many and many
a long day.

A considerable period elapsed, during which Eudæmon grew apace in stature and in knowledge.
He not only studied the many books of magic lore
left to him, but he also learnt marvellous lessons from
Nature herself. In his lonely isolation he had leisure
to attend to what our common mother is ready to
teach us all, would we but tarry awhile in our busy
lives and hearken to her still small voice.

Separated by his birth and dwelling-place from
mankind in general, Eudæmon strove to benefit the
few he could befriend. The island people, as a rule,
rarely beheld him. But in sickness or trouble they
ever turned (tremblingly, it is true) to the Castle gate,
where they waited while the trusty Donald apprised
his master of the presence of the suppliants without.

Strange cures were wrought by the simple remedies Eudæmon compounded from the various herbs
and minerals his mother had shown to him, or with
which his studies had rendered him familiar. To
seek these herbs at a propitious time, the youth
issued from the Castle at dead of night, with his
faithful Luachan, and traversed the hills till break
of day, when, wearied, and full of sleep, he often,
on his return, passed the daylight hours in repose.

He was, moreover, a keen and unerring marks-
man, swift and sure of foot, and of iron nerve.
The shuddering Highlanders sometimes marked his
eager pursuit of the wild goats, which at that time
abounded in the island. Master and hound seemed
alike dauntless and fearless in the chase, and whether
from his early love of climbing, or from his mixed
descent, it is hard to say, but it is very certain
that Eudæmon and his dog were often seen scrambling across the beetling crags that overhung the
sea, in places where no human foot has trodden
before or since. He and Lùachan also knew where
the golden eagle built her eyrie. He even caught
and tamed a young nestling, which loved Castle
Brochel as its home, and would only feed from her
master's hand. With Donald's assistance moreover
he had constructed a rude boat, in which they went
forth occasionally to seek a portion of their subsist-
ence by fishing.

Passionately fond of companionship, and denied
that of his own fellows, Eudæmon, by dint of long
perseverance, collected around him a motley variety
of animals. Tame seals lived on the rocks below
his dwelling. In perfect security around and beneath
the Castle walls roosted and nested a perfect colony
of sea-birds. A little flock of goats amply supplied
the three inhabitants with milk ; while conies, blue

P

hares, domestic fowls of various kinds, and last, but not least, serpents, from time immemorial the emblems of wisdom, throve and multiplied within the precincts or in close proximity to Eudæmon's home.

In those remote times, it is not surprising that old Donald, with his queer, misshapen figure, and solitary glaring eye, his youthful master, so wise beyond his years, and even the poor collie Luachan, whose sagacity was far above the average, were one and all regarded with some degree of superstitious mistrust.

It was said, that in the little turret chamber, highest in the Castle wall, from which at night streamed forth a ruddy ray of light, Eudæmon held converse with visitants from another world, and that many a storm was concocted and wafted abroad by their dark agency.

While the young student strove anxiously to benefit the cases of sickness brought before him —sometimes, indeed, spending whole nights wrestling face to face with death, by the side of some poor peasant's bed—a few of the people were ungrateful enough to attribute his cures to magic art and to an unholy alliance with the powers of darkness. Some humble hearts, however, throbbed with responsive gratitude at the very mention of his name; and there was one mother who, though the King of Terrors had proved too powerful for his adversary's skill, never forgot the tear of sorrow that fell from the young man's eye, as, after long watching and many unavailing remedies, her bonnie bairn breathed out her innocent life in Eudæmon's arms.

His fame was gradually bruited abroad, and as years rolled on he became widely known as "the Enchanter of the North."

From all the surrounding districts the inhabitants flocked in boats to seek his advice. Fishermen asked for charms, to ensure a successful summer. Ere the sailors put to sea, they deemed themselves lucky if they could secure one of Eudæmon's so-called "amulets" against disaster. These were, in reality, small bags manufactured and sold (in private) by the one-eyed seneschal, whose master would have been sorely displeased, had he discovered the chaffering trade driven in "charms" by the cunning old man, who thus rivalled Gehazi of ancient times!

Now it chanced that about this time there dwelt on the Lowland Borders, a King and Queen of Clutha, whose only daughter was afflicted with a terrible misfortune.

The Princess Miranda was beautiful as the day. Her parents, who had long lived in the bonds of matrimony without possessing any children, felt inexpressible joy as they welcomed their sweet little girl into the world. Bells were rung and bonfires lighted upon all the hills on either side of the river Clutha, which ran through her father's domains. Everything went on propitiously, until, in an hour of woe, it was discovered that the infant Princess could not speak!

This dire and unexpected calamity threw the whole Court, and indeed the nation at large, into deep distress. All, both high and low, heartily sympathized with the grief-stricken parents. Philosophers, astrologers, physicians, and wise women were each consulted in their turn ; but all, alas! in vain. At last, in desperation, the unhappy parents even offered the hand and dowry of their daughter as a reward to any man who should be fortunate enough to set her tongue at liberty.

Years rolled on. The King and Queen were disappointed in their hope of other offspring. Their feelings became more and more bitter, as they reflected on the confusion that would inevitably arise, should they die, and the dumb Miranda be called to the throne. They feared, with reason, that wicked men might take advantage of the Princess's helpless condition, and wrest the crown and kingdom from her hands.

Ambassadors from many surrounding countries

were attracted by the beauty of Miranda's portraits, carefully and widely disseminated by her prudent mother. One by one, however, these envoys dis. appeared, on finding that the beautiful Princess, though possessed of every other charm, was dumb.

The King and Queen, to soften as far as possible their child's misfortune, gave orders that her play-mates and attendants were always to address her in writing. All at court were told to conceal from the Princess as much as possible the difference be-tween her own condition and that of the maidens around her.

The consequence of these ill-judged regulations was that the Court of Clutha became almost as silent as the grave. Even musical instruments— with the exception of the fife and the drum, neces-sary for military and state occasions—were com-pletely banished from the precincts of the palace, to save the youthful Miranda from discovering what it was to be without a voice for singing or speaking.

Under these circumstances it is not to be won-dered at that foreign courtiers found King Mur-doch's Court insufferably dull, especially as the lovely Princess, herself a prey to melancholy, spent the greater part of her time amid the wild moors and glens surrounding her father's castle, where at least she could uninterruptedly listen to the sounds

of Nature. The sweet singing, or startled calls of
the various birds, the rippling and murmuring of
the rushing waters, the ceaseless humming of the
insects, the sighing of the wind among the leaves
and branches of the trees—each and all she heard
and learnt to love.

Among the ambassadors referred to there was one
representing a Prince, whose ardour could not be
checked by the Princess's cruel misfortune.

Some short time before the period of which we
speak, the King and Queen of Clutha, accompanied
by their daughter, paid a visit to the Queen's sister,
a powerful Princess in Ireland.

Left early a widow, Queen Hildegonda had long
since forgotten all the softer charms of womanly
nature. Forced, when hardly more than a girl herself, to protect her infant son, Prince Eochy, the heir
to his father's wide domains, from the continued
assaults, not only of neighbouring chieftains, but also
of rebellious and usurping subjects, she had become
a very amazon. By her wise and judicious regency,
she had secured a peaceful rule for her son. But
when the time came for him to take his rightful place,
the proud mother could not bring herself to resign
the reins of power. Eochy, as effeminate and weak
as his mother was masculine and daring, willingly
yielded to her the responsibilities of government,

and passed his life in idle poetical dreams and frivolous amusements.

On Miranda's appearance, however, the susceptible Prince, as might have been expected, was captivated by his fair cousin's matchless beauty. In vain the maiden's parents bestowed upon Eochy their own approval. In vain the enamoured youth besought his mother to favour his suit. Hildegonda, inexorable and unyielding, declared that no dumb Queen should ever reign in Cashel, and commanded her son to retire to a distant province until his relatives had departed.

Murdoch and his spouse lost no time in quitting with their daughter these inhospitable shores. When they once more reached home, they were roused by Hildegonda's insulting behaviour to attempt still more earnestly to unravel the cruel mystery that bound the lips of their beautiful daughter.

In the meantime the hapless Eochy utterly failed to make any deep impression on his cousin's heart. He languished in all the misery of unrequited love, and continually breathed forth his lamentations in cdes and poems such as this:—

> " What though I be King of the Emerald Isle,
>   And my Court in its Castle with beauty be bright,
> To me it were brighter by far could the smile
>   Of the one I remember but gladden my sight.

" Ah yes ! I remember too faithfully yet
    That evening and all its enchantment to me,
· That silvery wreath I shall never forget,
    That star-spangled Maiden from over the sea.

" I had gazed on the snow-mantled vale as it lay
    In the silence of morning all spotless and white,
And I wished that unchanged the fair prospect would stay
    To delight me, no sunset, no evening, no night :

" But the evening would come, and with evening a glow
    So rosy and glorious and delicate shone,
Bright Phœbus, I vowed, must be wooing the snow,
    And I envied the sweet bridal blush he had won.

" I had gazed on the ocean so calm and serene,
    The breezes seemed hushed to be watching her sleep:
I whispered, could mortal imagine a scene
    More sweet than the peacefully slumbering deep?

" But the sun shining forth, on a sudden there grew
    Such a change, every ripple seemed laughing and glad,
Such a dazzling and glancing of golden and blue,
    I wondered it e'er could seem slumbering or sad.

" Sweet, when I had met thee the charms were united,
    The snow of that morn of that evening the glow
On thy cheek and thy brow,—Oh, I would they were plighted
    To me, as they were 'twixt the sun and the snow !

" And the laughter of ocean I saw in thine eyes,
    When a light from within had enkindled the flame,—
How I wished I knew what might be worthy the prize
    Those fair joyous glances for ever to claim !

" Let them boast that the daughters of Erin are bright,
    Let them sing their wild songs to the maids of Kildare ;
I'll sing, and I'll sing till they own I am right,
    There's a maiden in Scotland, a maiden more fair !"

When Miranda received by special messengers.

these and other similar effusions from the love-sick Eochy, she conjured up before her mind's eye the sandy locks, the unmeaning grey eyes, the ungraceful lounging figure, and the good-natured but facile countenance of the effeminate young Prince. She smiled to herself as she contrasted him with the ideal hero of her imagination, sprung from the well-remembered tales of the dark impetuous sea-kings of the north.

About this time the King and Queen heard of and resolved to consult the oracle at Cumbrae for their afflicted daughter. They hoped to gain from the shrine of the far-famed lion some insight into her dark destiny.

After they had offered the richest gifts, and personally invoked its mysterious aid, the oracle returned the following enigmatical answer to their prayers, nor could the utmost entreaties gain from it any further explanation :—

> " The Eagle that soared o'er Kyle Akin's swift strait,
> Hath wooed and hath won the soft dove for his mate;
> Affliction hath wearied affection to rest,
> And cold is the heart in that mother's fond breast.

> " The strange freaks of fate in one web have entwined,
> What the Eaglet and maiden alone can unbind ;
> By chequered adventure, and music's soft thrill,
> The compass shall aid in deliverance from ill.
> Arise and speed northward, the prophet hath spoken,
> Miranda's long silence by love shall be broken."

Enquiries were at once set on foot regarding the mysterious "Eaglet" mentioned by the oracle. It was discovered that a certain Enchanter of the north named Eudæmon, was sometimes called "the Tamer of the Golden Eagle," and was indeed by some supposed to have been reared in an eagle's nest. The hopes of the afflicted parents rose high as they listened to the wondrous tales told of the great Enchanter's power.

A gorgeous galley was forthwith prepared wherein the King and Queen with their daughter embarked, taking with them but a slender retinue, for it was rumoured that the wise man lived secluded from his fellows, and would not brook intrusion. A small flotilla to protect and watch over the royal vessel received orders to hover near, but on no account to come within sight of the wizard's castle, for fear of exciting his displeasure.

The voyage was long and perilous. Autumn had already far advanced. Equinoctial gales lashed the western sea into swelling billows, so that after struggling with difficulty up the stormy sounds of Mull and Sleat, the galley containing the Princess and her parents, at length became separated from all her convoys and stranded on the western coast of Raasay. The King, Queen, and Princess barely escaped with their lives; their attendants also were saved, but the choice treasures intended to propitiate the Enchanter were carried by mermaidens as spoil to the palace of the sea gods.

Drenched and perishing with cold, the unfortunate voyagers were rescued from the bleak shore, and hospitably entertained by the poor islanders, who little imagined that in these storm-beaten mariners they beheld the great King Murdoch, the wise Queen Margaret, and the unfortunate Princess Miranda.

It is true that the Queen, with that prudence and forethought which occasionally guided her smaller actions, had caused her chief dresser to sew their three second-best Crowns into a small package, which was still attached to her belt and concealed by her dress, but with this exception (which seemed of little practical use), nothing remained to mark the exalted station of the royal wanderers.

Great, however, was their satisfaction to find that they were shipwrecked on the *very* island where the Enchanter of the North had his lonely abode. They made many enquiries concerning him, and heard that his actions were beneficent, and his cures almost certain. They were, nevertheless, warned by the islanders that nothing more excited his indignation than the presence of many people at his gate. He had, indeed, been known to refuse aid altogether to their comrades, who, from superstition or folly, had gone in numbers to beset the Castle entrance.

It was now therefore customary among these simple yet considerate people, to convoy the suppliant within a short distance of Castle Brochel. They then remained waiting on the hill above, while their fellow descended and returned. So universal had this practice become, that a small shieling was gradually thrown together stone upon stone by islanders waiting on different occasions for some friend below; exposed for the time being to all the inclemency of that most variable climate.

Here then the King and Queen waited while their beloved daughter (bearing with her the white and silver tablets by means of which she was wont to communicate with others) was told to present herself at the wicket-gate of the Castle. She was moreover given money wherewith to propitiate the much-dreaded Donald—the stern one-eyed guardian of the Enchanter's abode.

It was one of those days in early November when the exquisite "Indian summer" sometimes casts a perfect halo of beauty over the "soft" north-western atmosphere of Scotland. The little group paused . on the eminence immediately commanding the tall gaunt building below. In reality, the Castle top was above them; but to gain access to

its portals, it was necessary to descend to a considerable depth, and then remount by a narrow causeway to its frowning door.

The afternoon sun gilded the turrets with golden
radiance, beyond slumbered the blue rippling waters,
calm and treacherous, giving no sign of their cruel
strength. Far in the distance like faint clouds, lay
the curving outline of the Highland hills, tipped with
snow, and dimly visible as they blushed pink in the
parting rays of the monarch of day.

The last farewell spoken, and the afflicted child
tenderly pressed to her parents' hearts; the gentle
Miranda, with slow footstep, descended the fateful
path.

In the meantime Eudæmon, by his consultations
with the stars (an art partly taught him by his
mother, who had carried away for her child, when
she escaped from Valbiorn's terrible dwelling, strange
manuscripts of astrological and magic lore), had become aware of the impending visit of a being
whose fate was mysteriously connected with his
own.

He was absorbed in abstruse calculations when
Luachan, suddenly pricking up his ears, and impatiently scratching at the door, gave notice that
some stranger approached the castle. On his master's
unfastening the latch, the fleet animal made one

bound, and disappeared down the narrow staircase, while the magician heard old Donald's querulous quavering tones raised high, as if to refuse admittance. Quick as thought Eudæmon sprang lightly after his dog, and entered the hall, where an astonishing sight greeted his bewildered eyes.

A maiden of surpassing beauty had evidently made her way into the Castle when the seneschal was off his guard. She now stood irresolute in the centre of the apartment. Luachan, contrary to immemorial custom (for, as a rule, he was surly to strangers), gambolled around the beautiful unknown with extravagant gestures of affectionate welcome, while the one-eyed Donald, shaking in his hoary wrath, poured forth an incomprehensible flood of Celtic indignation.

Eudæmon rushed forward, and signed to the old man to hold his peace, then turning to his fair visitant, he gently asked her will. Miranda, amazed to behold in the dreaded Enchanter no ancient, withered seer, no venerable prophet, as she had anticipated, but the dark-haired ideal of her wild dreams about the sea kings of the north, remained rooted to the spot, ashamed of her wilful intrusion and covered with burning blushes.

Eudæmon gazed, like one entranced, on his mysterious guest. Her long golden tresses, and her exquisite beauty of feature and form, startled the recluse of the rock. At first he almost imagined her to be of angelic extraction ; but her unmistakeable confusion betrayed mortal birth, and in bolder tones the Enchanter again requested her to make known her wishes.

The Princess, seized with sudden terror, looked towards the door by which she had entered, but it was closed, and Donald stood before it, glaring at her angrily with his solitary orb. In her distress her hand involuntarily sought the tablets, where she now remembered that she herself had written the following explanatory lines, during her long and tedious journey from the south. With a bashful half-smile, therefore, she unclasped the ivory pages from her side, and timidly handed them to the Magician, who there beheld inscribed these lines.

> " Hearken mighty seer, Eudæmon,
> Tamer of the golden Eagle,
> Aquila the golden Eagle,
> Hearken, merciful Eudæmon,
> Measurer of the raging tempest,
> Of the unseen raging tempest,
> Hearken to a lowland maiden,
> To the silent maid Miranda
> To the sad Princess Miranda.

> " I am come from Clutha's waters,
> From its distant tranquil waters,

Where through changing isles of sunshine,
Looms the ocean, where the west wind
Rustles through the matted foliage,
Or, with a delicious shiver,
Sweeps along the silver beeches.
I am come to sea-girt Raasay,
To the wave-washed island Raasay,
To the storm-swept, rugged Raasay,
I have braved Kintyre's wild headlands—
Braved its mountain-rising billows,
Braved dark Cory-Vreckan's whirlpool,
Braved the fortress of Artornish,
Braved the fabled Ardnamurchan,
Ship-engulfing Ardnamurchan,
Braved the blasts from Scuir-na-gillean,
But to plead with thee for succour,
Aid against the fell enchantment,
Terrible unknown enchantment,
Which hath bound my lips to silence—
Gloomy unresponsive silence.
Maidens' mouths were made for singing,
Song and laughter are their sunshine ;
Cheering thus the world around them,
Wakening mirth with voice melodious.
Pity, then ! oh, great Enchanter !
Pity the poor spell-bound Princess,
Silent, sorrowful, dumb maiden,
And with pity give assistance,
Read the tale she cannot tell thee,
Charm the woes no sighs can cure."

Eudæmon perused the tablets with eager attention more than once, then, turning a keen, piercing eye on Miranda, he exclaimed.

"Princess ! I do not now hear of your misfortune

for the first time. I knew that you and your parents were in search of me and of my castle. During my researches and observations I have discovered that the conjunction of stars at your birth left one unfavourable moment. This was taken advantage of by Valbiorn to avenge upon your innocent lips a grudge he owed to your father, having been, in days gone by, an unsuccessful suitor for your mother's hand.

"By much careful study of the heavens I have ascertained that the enchantment can only be dissolved by my aid and that under very difficult conditions. Rest assured, however, that no effort on my part shall be wanting to set you free. But," continued Eudæmon, bending low before Miranda, "will your parents consent to remain under my humble roof a while, since what we must go through together will take days, if not weeks, to accomplish?"

The Princess joyfully clasped her hands, and while tears of joy ran down her fair cheeks at the prospect of deliverance, she inclined her head over and over again, to intimate that her parents would thankfully accept Eudæmon's welcome invitation.

The Enchanter now offered his hand to Miranda, and while Luachan testified his delight by bounding around them, led her through the Castle gate and accompanied her in search of the King and Queen. With all the unreasonableness of human nature, these potentates advancing to meet them, half expected to hear their daughter already speaking. They graciously accosted Eudæmon, however, and anxiously listened to his explanations.

It was finally arranged that the Queen and her daughter, with their solitary waiting-maid, (much to Donald's disgust), should be installed in a part of the Castle now never used, but where were still to be seen, when the doors were unlocked, the last traces of the gentle Bragela's feminine occupations· The islanders cheerfully lent what aid they could, and King Murdoch with his attendant was permanently fixed in the small shieling on the hill. It was impossible to accommodate him in the Castle, for though lofty, its proportions were narrow and cramped. Except to sleep therefore he very seldom left the precincts of Eudæmon's dwelling.

For several days and nights the Enchanter shut himself up alone in his high turret, examining dusty old volumes, and reading the heavens, by the aid of an instrument he himself had constructed. At the end of that time he emerged from his solitary chamber, descending with eager rapid step to join his guests at their evening meal. He bore under his arm a small box and a piece of board roughly marked in squares of two colours. His dark features wore an expression of anxious excitement.

No sooner had the last traces of the repast been cleared away than Eudæmon placed his board upon the table. Opening the box he then displayed to the Princess's delighted gaze a number of little men of various sizes and shapes. These were in fact neither more nor less than a set of chessmen which he had laboriously carved in wood with his own hands, and stained in two different colours, having ascertained the mode of using them from the careful study of ancient manuscripts.

Long before the Princess Miranda appeared in Raasay, Eudæmon had known and pondered over the mystic answer returned to her parents by the Cumbrae oracle. He diligently sought among his mother's ancient volumes of magic lore for some solution of the phrase "chequered adventure." At length he came upon the description of the ancient game of chess illustrated by rough drawings.

His attention was at once arrested by discovering that this game must be played upon a "chequered" board. After careful research he finally resolved to make the trial. It took him, however, a considerable time to fashion the various pieces from the old pictures he possessed.

The Princess, her countenance lit up with curiosity and interest, was soon seated at the little table opposite the Enchanter. Several evenings were spent in teaching her the various moves of the different pieces, and explaining to her the rules of the game.

Eudæmon was fully aware that only one hour during the twenty-four was available for the purpose of disenchantment.

Some evenings later the King and Queen, already grown somewhat sleepy, nodded drowsily in their chairs. The faithful Luachan lay between his master and the fair young guest, whose bright eyes gleamed with unwonted animation. Then the dark Enchanter arising from his seat trimmed the torch above their heads, and prepared, at midnight, to play in earnest the mystic game, so fraught with meaning to the afflicted Princess.

Miranda sat in an old-fashioned chair of curiously carved wood. Her white dress and her fair tresses reflected the flickering light, thus giving some brightness to the lofty hall, whose gloomy proportions were but partially revealed by the blazing fire and the fitful glare of the torch. The most profound silence reigned in the chamber, only broken by the cheerful crackling of the firewood or an occasional snore from the slumbering King.

Fully instructed in the moves by Eudæmon during the previous nights, the Princess and the Enchanter played an interesting game. He had cast aside his long upper robe of black velvet and showed the tightly fitting red under-suit which set off his active form to greatest advantage. He placed himself on a somewhat ricketty "creepie," for the unwonted number of guests had used up all his available chairs. As he bent eagerly forward the ruddy light fell on his swarthy face, and his small closely cropped, though curly black head. His burning eyes fixed alternately on the game, and on his silent opponent, seemed to pierce through all they surveyed.

The hour wore on, they exchanged several pieces. Eudæmon then moving a bishop, placed his antagonist's king in "check." He uttered the prophetic word. Miranda, thoroughly absorbed, took up her King, and was about to place him within range of her enemy's Queen. The Enchanter gently motioned her hand aside, pointing to his own piece in explanation.

At this moment Miranda broke into such silvery peals of laughter, that Luachan, affrighted, sprang barking from his resting place. Eudæmon in his surprise and delight moved suddenly and upset the whole board incontinently on the floor, ruining the game. Queen Margaret starting up, rushed across the hall.

She first held her child at arm's length as if to examine
into and convince herself of her identity, then clasping her tightly to her heart, shed tears of gladness
over her laughing daughter.   It was indeed evident
that the "chequered adventure" had fulfilled its
mission, and broken the first link in the silent
Miranda's chain of enchantment.

The excited parents knew not how to express their
feelings of gratitude, but listened in wondering astonishment to Miranda's ringing peals of laughter, as,
enraptured with her newly gained accomplishment,
she danced round the hall, accompanied by Luachan,
who vied with her in gambols of ecstatic joy.   Eudæmon had never before beheld anything more graceful than the young Princess appeared to him in all
her unconscious beauty of movement.

Inspired by a sudden desire to emulate and join
in her mirthful steps, he stretched forth his hand as
she passed him ; she swiftly caught it, and drew
him merrily on ; thus maid, master, and dog
together paced a wild impromptu measure of
delight.

Donald, hastening in to ascertain the cause of this
unusual commotion, gazed around, rubbed his solitary eye, and looked again and again.   Where was
the gloomy Eudæmon, the dreaded Enchanter of the
North ?   The youth heretofore so staid and reserved

now flushed and laughing, pirouetted round the bewildered old man with the smiling maiden. Together
they clapped their hands at his amazement.

But now the Queen, with the dignity of manner
that she well knew how to assume, bade her daughter
remember who and what she was. Forgetting her
late gratitude to their benefactor, she swept haughtily
from the apartment, followed by her husband and
her unwilling child. Miranda's pleading eyes, however, gave Eudæmon the thanks he most cared to
receive, and entirely obliterated from his mind all
thought of resentment against her uncertain parents.
At the same time he determined to take no further
steps until the King and Queen themselves again
spoke of their daughter's affliction.

Several days elapsed. The character of the Castle
was completely changed. The hitherto hermit like
Eudæmon felt impelled to try and elicit again those
silvery peals of laughter that rang on his ear with
such a curious thrill of pleasure. Nor was he unsuccessful in his efforts. Again and again the old
walls re-echoed with the welcome sound. The Enchanter himself felt once more a boy as he played
long games of chess with Miranda, or pointed out
to her his numerous pets and their diverse habits.
The Princess, however, was admonished to keep
carefully within her mother's sight ; she wast herefore

unable to scramble with him as he wished among the wild hills and cliffs around.

But the time flew swiftly by, and at length one morning the King and Queen craved an audience of their young host. Laying aside all traces of their late assumption of majesty they humbly entreated him to strive to work out still farther their daughter's cure.

Eudæmon listened in silence, fixing on them his piercing dark eye, until they moved uneasily beneath his searching glance. "I am esteemed worthy to aid in your child's disenchantment," he answered sternly, "but am too much beneath her in your eyes to tread with her the mazy measures of the dance, or to join in her everyday pursuits."

King Murdoch and his wife eagerly disclaimed any idea of making so ungenerous a return for his kindness. At length Eudæmon (who completely saw through their shallow minds, and only spoke to obtain more freedom for their daughter) promised to continue his lucubrations.

That evening for the first time since her death, he drew from a deep recess the dust-covered harp that had once quivered in responsive melody beneath the musical touch of his fair young mother. Miranda and the Queen curiously examined the quaint instrument, and helped to disentangle and divest it of its broken strings. Eudæmon, who had often studied its mechanism, brought forth new strings he himself had manufactured, and showed Miranda where and how they should be placed.

Several evenings passed in putting the harp to rights, then the Princess under Eudæmon's magical tuition strove to place aright upon it her slender fingers. Morning, noon, and night Miranda strove to play the melodies that ever floated before her mind's eye as sung to her by Eudæmon, who placed beside her scrolls, on which the words of the songs were written out.

One of them ran thus:

Thou speak'st of to-morrow, yet seemest to sigh,
And something there gleams like a tear in thine eye,
But though the sweet days of our converse are o'er,
The friendship that binds us shall cease nevermore.

When music entrancing shall steal on thine ear,
And songs shall be sung thee thou lovest to hear,
Oh, may one wild note of my harp seem to thrill,
And recall to thee one who remembers thee still.

And ever amid the dark shadows of life,
When faint from the battle or weary with strife,
Ah! then shall arise like the sun through a shower,
The remembrance of all we have felt in this hour.

When moonlight around thee shall flood the pale sea,
May thoughts of the north come like visions to thee,
And remind thee of hours when we once used to stray,
By the ocean's dark verge at the close of the day.

Roll onwards, roll onwards, thou swift flowing Clyde,
Yet may our loved friends ne'er resemble thy tide,
But changeless and steadfast look back through long years,
To the parting that left us in silence and tears.

This song, which Eudæmon had himself composed, and set to an old tune, was an especial favourite of Miranda's. She made the Enchanter sing it over again and again ; though, strange to say, the master who taught her fair hands to stray over the harp, could not himself draw one sound from its capricious chords. The Princess, however, soon became enabled to accompany all his songs, every day she learnt some new, and to her more entrancing, melody. For it will be remembered that her parents had hitherto, through mistaken affection, carefully kept all music from her knowledge.

The black and gold harp, which Eudæmon and Miranda had together tuned and restored, formed a beautiful contrast to the white flowing robes and the fair arms of the young Princess. Her long tresses bound only by the pale blue snood of the Scottish maiden, waved around her. As she raised her eyes to watch every motion of Eudæmon's mouth, she gave one the idea of an inspired being, from whose very finger-tips emanated the soul of melody. Thus they often sat late into the night, drinking in sweet sounds, and poring together over poor Bragela's old manuscripts. Meanwhile Miranda's parents, closely guarding as they thought their precious daughter, hardly suspected that, while engaged in finding a tongue, she might hopelessly lose her heart.

At last, one evening Eudæmon for the hundredth time sang again that verse beginning

When music entrancing shall steal on thine ear.

Just as he reached the end, Miranda suddenly, as if by an irresistible impulse, opened her lips. With wonderful pathos, and in a voice which seemed to the young man the sweetest that could sound on earth, she finished the line :—

Recall to thee one who remembers thee still.

Amazed at her own daring, and astonished by her unwonted power, the fair songstress started blushing from her seat. In an uncontrollable burst of emotion she rushed weeping from the chamber. Queen Margaret, unable to believe it was her dumb child's voice she had heard give utterance to such melodiously thrilling notes, rose also from her chair, and cast an eager inquiring glance upon Eudæmon. Himself overcome with emotion, the Enchanter did not trust his voice to speak, but merely bowed his head ; then, filled with yearning sympathy for the strangely-afflicted Princess, he opened the outer door of the hall, and hastily stepped forth on to the turreted court that overhung the shore.

It was a night of exquisite beauty—the water, calm as a mirror, stretched its dark amplitude between the solitary watcher and the far mainland of the Rossshire hills. Orion, in all his resplendent grandeur, sparkled before him, and seemed in silent majesty to rebuke the feverish turbulence of the Enchanter's too human heart. High and cold above his head the silver crescent moon travelled dreamily across the vaulted heaven, and, as if to remind Eudæmon of her presence, cast her glittering likeness into the deep ocean's embrace, far below his feet. One by one, in gentle crashing cadence, the tiny wavelets broke beneath the Castle wall.

Insensibly soothed and quieted by nature's wondrous charm, the philosopher leant his burning head upon his hands, and absently gazed seawards.

Suddenly the casement above was thrown violently open, and Queen Margaret, in terror-stricken accents, besought his speedy aid.

He re-entered the hall. It was empty and desolate, the torch was extinguished, the fire flickered low upon the hearth. He heard a confused murmur of voices, and recognised Luachan's muffled howl of distress in the distance.

Following the sounds, he hastened up the narrow

stair, and found a sorrowful group at the door of the room set apart for the Queen and her daughter. Pressing past Murdoch and Donald, and angrily motioning to Luachan to be silent, the Enchanter himself uttered a cry of anguish as his eye fell upon Miranda's death-like form. Stretched upon the rude bed, with her dishevelled tresses tangled around her pale face, on which were still the traces of tears, the poor Princess looked as if she had for ever closed her eyes to mortal scenes.

On Eudæmon's entrance, the unhappy mother rushed towards him, exclaiming, "Save her, save her ! restore our darling ; all shall be as you wish, if but you bring her back to life !" A deep red flush mounted to the Enchanter's very temples as the Queen, fervently pressing his hand, whispered these words, fraught with so much meaning, into his willing ear. But he needed no promised guerdon to urge him to his labour of love.

Kneeling beside the low couch, he vainly chafed Miranda's ice-cold hands. He listened over her heart —not even the feeblest flutter rewarded his strained attention. He placed a tiny polished tablet over her parted lips ; its surface remained clear and unsullied by mortal breath. A sudden thought struck terror to his soul. He turned a keen glance on the mother's face ; her eye fell before his ; a guilty blush suffused her cheek. "You have forgotten my earnest charge," he cried, "and now it may be too late to save your child."

At this moment the magic cock was heard through the open casement crowing loudly in the castle yard. Eudæmon flew to the window and anxiously peered into the night. Right above his head, and threateningly suspended directly over the Castle, was a meteor of unwonted size and brilliancy. He fell on his knees where he stood, and stretching forth his arms silently implored Heavenly protection against the powers of evil. Again and again the ball of fire grew lurid and glowing, as though it were about to descend and bury them beneath burning ruins, but each time Chanticleer's warning voice sounded cheerfully near at hand, and at length the red globe, with a loud hissing noise, fell prone and harmless into the dark ocean depths.

Relieved from the pressing danger without, Eudæmon now turned to the sorrow within.

Since the appearance of the Royal wanderers upon the island, he had held many private conversations with the Queen concerning her daughter's disenchantment.

The anxious mother over and over again informed him that the dearest object of their heart, in seeking to free their child from the spell which bound her, was that Miranda should be united in marriage with some powerful monarch, who would aid her, in due time, to rule over her own somewhat troublous kingdom of Clutha.

She little knew that Eudæmon was intimately acquainted with their past history, nor did she suspect that he was aware of the vow made by herself and King Murdoch in bygone days. Wearied by vain endeavours to accomplish their daughter's disenchantment, they had then solemnly bound themselves by an oath to bestow Miranda's hand on the man who should succeed in releasing her spell-bound voice.

During the long years which had elapsed since Bragela's death, Valbiorn's hard heart had gradually softened towards her only child. He knew of the promised reward. From afar he watched with keen suspicion the movements of the King and Queen. He foresaw that Eudæmon would love Miranda, if fate brought them together. For his sake he resolved to help the Princess, but, at the same time, he determined that the gift of speech should only be restored to render her a more fitting bride for his son.

When, therefore, the young Enchanter retired to his turret chamber, he often held secret interviews with his dread father, and succeeded in gaining a pledge of assistance from Valbiorn. But Eudæmon feared that if his vindictive parent once suspected Queen Margaret's intentions, he would not only refuse his aid altogether, but would become her deadliest foe.

Before the King and Queen set sail for the Highlands, she had resolved that their solemn oath should be buried in oblivion. She satisfied her conscience by lading their ship with precious gifts destined for the propitiation of the Enchanter.

Had Eudæmon been the ancient prophet she thought he was, he would probably have accepted golden rewards with delight. The treasures, however, never reached the island ; they were engulfed in the stormy ocean.

As soon as Miranda's mother saw Eudæmon, she perceived that his deep interest in her fair daughter might be turned to good account. She persuaded her husband to leave the matter in her hands, priding herself upon her powers of negociation.

Feeling instinctively the young man's innate delicacy of mind, the wily Queen took good care to enlist his sympathies for her afflicted child. At the same time she continually alluded to Miranda's exalted station, tacitly ignoring the possibility of a suitor for her hand whose pretensions were less than royal.

Eudæmon was wont to listen to her words with respectful courtesy, though occasionally his skill in necromancy stood him but in poor stead, when his rebel heart sent a crimson glow over his dark features. Still he invariably replied in measured tones that his own desires perfectly coincided with those of the maiden's parents ; that his chief wish was to promote the welfare and happiness of the young Princess, and to render her any assistance in his power. ·

Latterly, however, during the long hours spent at chess, in rambling about the Castle and its precincts, or in singing and playing over the harp, the good Queen's heart misgave her, and she took the somewhat bold step of directly warning her benefactor and host against engaging her daughter's affections.

Notwithstanding his powers of self-control, Eudæmon had to pause a moment and curb the hasty impulse of anger, ere he answered in low, husky tones,

" Madam, for your child's sake, I have embarked upon the perilous undertaking of striving to free her from the well-woven spell which for nineteen long years has bound her lips to silence, and cast a blight over her young life.

" The Princess Miranda's happiness is at stake. I persevere, therefore, in my endeavours to aid her. Absorbed, however, in a struggle to the death with

R

the dread powers of darkness, I have now little time
to regard her in any other light but that of the ill-
fated victim of enchantment. I will, nevertheless,
warn you that your child is innocence itself. Her
spirit must inevitably be sorely tried during coming
events, and very little more might serve to unhinge
her mind. Take heed, therefore, that you suffer no
word of what has passed between us to reach her
unsuspecting ears.

"I have no desire to interfere with the brilliant
destiny you have mapped out for your daughter,
or to tempt her to disobey her parents.

"But though you ignore the vow you took upon
yourself in less hopeful days, it is remembered by
one who never forgets. Within and around this
Castle exists an invisible agency ; nor can what passes
here be kept from the knowledge of a mightier power
than mine.

"More I dare not say. I have no wish to stand
before you as a suppliant. For the present, I pray
you only to remember that you are my honoured ˎ
guests, and that my time and my thoughts are alike
devoted to your service."

As he spoke, the excited and wounded Enchanter
drew himself to his full height. Indignant lightning
flashed from his eyes, controlled passion vibrated
in his voice.

The Queen, frightened and conscience-stricken, gazed bewildered upon Eudæmon, as, with an abrupt reverence, he turned and quitted her presence. For many hours he disappeared from the neighbourhood of the Castle, and several days elapsed before he regained his wonted equanimity of bearing.

On this eventful night, therefore, the young Seer heard with mingled feelings the terrified mother's significant words. But there was now no time for further explanation. When the threatened attack from without had been warded off, the Enchanter turned from the turret window and exclaimed, "Away with you all; you must quit this chamber and leave me alone with the maiden and her mother, if it be not already too late to attempt to restore her ebbing life."

Thereupon he strode to the threshold, and assuming an air of majesty they had never before remarked, he waved them in silence from the apartment.

No sooner had they all quitted the room, than Eudæmon drew the bolt across the door, and approaching the Queen, who hung weeping over her lifeless daughter, he thus sternly addressed her :—

"You have neglected my warning, and by your heedless words have awakened a fresh struggle in the breast of this sorely tried · child. There remains but one chance of recalling her gentle spirit from the Valley of the Shadow of Death. But be assured, proud Queen, that though, for the sake of the Princess herself, I now lay bare before you the inmost secret of my heart; yet she shall never know, until she hears the truth from your lips, that for her alone that heart shall beat through time and through eternity."

So saying, the young Enchanter drew near Miranda's prostrate form. He threw himself on the floor beside her couch, and seizing her resistless hands, wildly pressed them in his own. Tenderly and reverently he addressed the insensible maiden in tones and words of fondest endearment. For long it seemed as though even the electric thrill of mortal love was powerless against the magic swoon into which the Princess had fallen on hearing for the first time her mother's strange accusing words.

At last Eudæmon (who held her hand in his as he fervently prayed for her restoration to life) fancied he perceived a feeble movement. He arose, and earnestly imprinting on his memory those features so sacred to him in their helpless repose, he retired to the window and there continued his prayer.

Meanwhile Miranda, quivering back to consciousness, imagined she heard a familiar voice addressing her in the wild tones of a passionate love hitherto unknown. A strange new pain shot into her innocent soul, and awoke her once more to play her part in this world's theatre.

She slowly opened her eyes, and looked around. By the light of the feeble lamp she gradually became aware of Eudæmon's presence, as he knelt near the open casement, through which faintly glimmered the first signs of approaching dawn. She stirred uneasily on her couch. The Enchanter arose from his answered prayer. Stepping across the chamber, he opened the door to the impatient watchers without. Before Queen Margaret could recover from her astonishment, or could indeed realize that her child was safe, Eudæmon was gone. He went out silently as the others entered. Calling Luachan, he departed thence with his faithful dog, to seek amid the solitudes of nature that peace which at present was denied him by his wildly throbbing bosom.

Many days elapsed before the Princess, shaken and confused by all she had gone through, again descended the stairs and approached once more the fated harp. From the moment in which her feelings had found vent in song, and escaping from the hall she had sought relief from tears in her lonely chamber, all seemed like a dream. Her mother's reproaches on discovering her strange agitation, her deep swoon, and the words she thought she had heard as she woke, each and all were regarded by her as the creatures of her own too vivid imagination.

Queen Margaret, already forgetting her renewed promises, and fondly caressing her child, never recurred to the past. The Enchanter, entering as before with energy into all that concerned Miranda's interests, looked and moved to the awe-struck eyes of the simple Princess an exalted being, free from the weaknesses or restless anxieties of mortal love.

Miranda's new power gave them all exquisite pleasure. She herself found rich stores of unimagined delight, as she poured forth her growing aspirations in floods of song. Strange to say, it was in singing alone that she gave utterance to her feelings. No spoken word as yet could pass the enchanted barrier of her lips.

A visible cloud sat upon Eudæmon's swarthy brow. He foresaw that Miranda's disenchantment could only be accomplished amid real dangers and difficulties, and his heart misgave him as he realized the faint trust that could be placed in the ready promises of the Queen.

Day after day elapsed without further adventure, no allusion was made to the remarkable words that had fallen from Miranda's mother when she was overwhelmed by the immediate danger of her child.

At length, one evening, after Miranda had retired weary to her couch, the young Seer set forth to her parents the only course to be pursued, if the Princess were ever to obtain the power of speech.

He explained to them that far away, in the mysterious halls of Thuisto, there existed a wondrous compass, with which Miranda's fate was closely connected. He told them, moreover, that with the aid of magic he could introduce himself, the Princess, and her mother into the weird abode of the sea-kings.

But to do this, and to escape in safety, silence and obedience were imperatively necessary. Before venturing on so serious a risk, he therefore solemnly entreated the Queen sooner to rest content with the partial disenchantment of her daughter, and to quit in peace his lonely abode, than to enter lightly upon this grave adventure. For when once within the enchanted precincts of Thuisto, if they transgressed ever so slightly, the rules laid down for their observance, they would draw down, not only upon himself—for which he little cared—but perchance upon Miranda, the fatal vengeance of the ever-watchful guardians of those submarine palaces.

Again and again the eager mother promised, nay, even swore to obey his strict injunctions, urging him to make the attempt. At last, with heavy foreboding, Eudæmon prepared to encounter the dangers of the coming expedition.

Miranda was told of the projected scheme. The Enchanter explained to her that in the submerged vaults of Thuisto she would probably first find the use of her voice in speech. He warned her, however, that she must endeavour to speak only when he bade her, and Queen Margaret was once more pledged to maintain strict silence.

The eventful night arrived. The poor forsaken king and the disconsolate dog Luachan (too intelligent to move from the shore where his beloved master bade him remain and guard the stranger), together strained their eyes from the wild beach below Castle Brochel, as the little boat containing the travellers became a faint speck on the starlit sea.

Eudæmon and the one-eyed Donald rowed their precious burden quickly on, until reaching a barren rock, the Enchanter sprang lightly on shore ; carefully handing out Queen Margaret and her daughter, he then bade the old man row home to the Castle and return again for them at day-break.

Hardly had the regular plash of Donald's retreating oars died away, before they became conscious that they were gradually sinking through the ocean. The broad, flat surface on which they stood afforded them ample footing, and though they heard, on either side, the swift rushing of the divided waters, not a drop touched them; not an oscillation disturbed their balance, as, supported and cheered by Eudæmon's friendly whispers, and fast clinging together, mother and daughter descended through the sea to unknown regions, enveloped in a darkness that might be felt.

Mindful of her plighted word, the Queen uttered no sound, but she bore very heavily upon the young Enchanter's arm, keeping him in constant uneasiness. At length a blinding flash of light smote on their dazzled eyes; the downward motion ceased, and the stone on which they stood sank to its resting-place with a loud clang.

As they became inured to the brightness, they beheld before, behind, around them on every side, as far as sight could reach, a vast labyrinth of arched and pillared cloisters, stretching into interminable ·distance, and lit by some mysteriously effulgent ray, which seemed to their bewildered gaze to proceed from the centre of a broader aisle, at one extremity of which they themselves stood.

Eudæmon, motioning them to follow, trod slowly the echoing pavement, and advanced towards the distant focus of light.

Now sounded forth music such as earthly ears have seldom heard. It was as if all the harmonies of

water's various movements swelled into one indescribable wave of translucent melody, that penetrated
soul and body with its enervating power. Relaxed in
every fibre by this weird influence, Eudæmon with
difficulty urged forward his drooping comrades. Prepared, however, to resist to the utmost the charms of
witchcraft, he drew forth his magic horn, and its
reviving fragrance quickly restored energy to their
unstrung frames.

Their interest also was freshly aroused by exquisite statues, which, almost endued with life, and
perfect in colouring, seemed to smile on them from
either side as they proceeded. They reached the
circle whence emanated the diverging rays of light.
Before them blazed a dazzling but empty throne.
From its midst shone those awe-inspiring beams.

Eudæmon uttered a low cry. There, beauteous
as he remembered her in his boyhood's early days,
but with a calm expression of perfect peace she had
never worn during her child's lifetime, in a marble
niche close beside the vacant seat, stood the lovely
Bragela. Her long golden tresses rippled over her
shoulders, her flowing robes half showed, half concealed her matchless shape, while her azure eyes,
with their heavily-fringed lids, fell fixed and cold on
the eager countenance of her son.

A moment he paused, half expectant, dreaming

that her loved spirit must awake and welcome him, but in that instant her last words flashed across his mind. He realized that Valbiorn's skill had only thus been able to immortalize the fair, soulless clay. He remembered once more why he had sought that dread abode, and he noted that Bragela's beautiful motionless hand pointed to a small amber pedestal, which at a few paces distant seemed to glow with lambent flame.

He approached : upon its summit lay the object of his search, the magic compass of the sea-kings, potent to work weal or woe. Turning to Miranda, he gently drew her forward, and placed the timid maiden over against himself on the southern side of the mystic pillar.

The whole of the magic compass quivered and shone with the appearance of red-hot metal, but Eudæmon whispered to the Princess that she must with a firm hand raise the needle from its place, and, turning towards the north, pronounce these words in an audible voice,

"As points the faithful needle to the pole."

Miranda stooped trembling over the flaming altar, but with gentle courage she took the fiery needle in her hand ; as she did so, she raised her eyes trustingly towards her guide, and moved a step nearer to him.

Here in the enchanted palace of his fathers, surrounded by mysterious influences, and excited by the anticipated victory over Miranda's spell, the youth for once forgot his careful self-command. He also advanced, and stretched out his eager hands to bound the needle's range.

In a low musical tone the Princess pronounced the fateful words; ere she finished, she leant insensibly forwards, and the needle almost touched the Enchanter's breast. Overcome with mingled emotions, Miranda, while she spoke, swayed visibly to and fro, and as if to support her, Eudæmon's arms fell on either side of her tottering figure.

At this moment the Queen, terribly discomposed, and forgetting in her displeasure every solemn promise she had made, rushed forward, loudly crying, " Misguided girl!" but ere she could continue her sentence, a tremendous peal of thunder shook the ground beneath their feet, and vibrated around them. An intensely lurid ray of light darted athwart the heretofore empty throne. To Queen Margaret's unspeakable dread, she beheld indistinctly amid the dazzling beams an awful form enthroned in fire. A rushing noise filled her ears, she became insensible, and as she did so, she seemed to fall prone through interminable depths.

*   *   *   *   *   *

It was long before she recovered her consciousness, but at last she was aroused by the sound of sweet singing,

" I would I were a little bird,
  To build upon his breast,
Or if I were a nightingale,
  To soothe my love to rest.
To gaze upon his tender eyes,
  All my reward should be,
For I love, I love, I love my love,
  Because my love loves me."

Opening her eyes with a shiver at the wild pathos of these tones, the Queen, by the chill bright light of the December sun, beheld her daughter, with Luachan beside her, seated on the beach of Raasay and twining pieces of damp sea-weed into her long hair.

Queen Margaret raised herself from the ground, and drew her hand across her brow. What had happened?

She herself lay on the grass close to the sea-shore; and near at hand Castle Brochel towered frowning into the morning sky. She called to her daughter. Miranda heeded not.

But now the sound of oars was heard, one-eyed Donald roughly grated his boat on the shingle, and scrambling out, asked the Queen somewhat gruffly how she came there.

Confused and distressed, she could give no satisfactory answer. Donald then recounted to her how he had been rowing for hours round and round the spot where they had landed the previous night, unable to discover any trace of the large flat rock on which they had disembarked. At last in despair he had returned to the Island.

When he observed Miranda and her mother on the shore he expected also to see Eudæmon near at hand. Disappointed in this hope, he now continued, pointing inland with his long, skinny finger. "I wadna say but the maister is in the Castle itsel'."

At this moment, however, the Princess approached them, singing, sadly,

> "But should it please the pitying powers,
>   To call him to the sky,
> I'll plead a guardian angel's charge,
>   Around my love to fly.
> To guard him from all danger,
>   How happy I should be,
> For I love, I love, I love my love,
>   Because my love loves me."

As she sang, Luachan uttered a melancholy howl. The perplexed seneschal looked from one to another in silent amazement, then muttering to himself, " It's no unco canny for the beast to howl that gate," he hastened, as fast as his withered limbs would permit, up the steep ascent to the Castle gate.

Meantime the Queen gazed fixedly on her daughter. What strange alteration had taken place in her beloved child? Those gentle blue eyes, wont to rest so placidly on all they surveyed, now restlessly turned from side to side, and never looked her straight in the face. Her busy fingers plucked nervously at the wet garlands she carried on her arms, and her lips moved ceaselessly, though no audible sound came from them.

"Miranda, my love," said the anxious mother, "how came we hither?" A look of unutterable woe troubled the maiden's face. She drew from her bosom a golden needle, and holding it towards the north, she exclaimed,

"As points the faithful needle to the pole."

Swinging the long slimy sea-weeds around her, she then suddenly gave a shrill laugh, and rushed up the castle hill, followed by Luachan, whose drooping ears and limp tail, seemed to the Queen's excited imagination prophetic of evil.

Stiff and sore in every limb from her unusual exposure, Queen Margaret raised herself from the ground and toiled slowly up the steep ascent.

Ere she reached the crest of the rocks upon which the Castle stood, the King came forth to meet her. In a terrible voice he cried—"What have you done to our child, to my darling Miranda?"

Thoroughly overcome with fatigue and misery, the poor Queen burst into tears, and Murdoch forgetting for the moment all save his wife's uncontrollable emotion, soothed her as best he could, and led her into the Castle hall.

Here she told her husband the strange events of the past night. She related their various adventures after Donald left them on the rock, and now, when too late, she bitterly lamented over her own hasty interference, and her imprudent words. She described how she had only time to perceive a being of noble and majestic mien seated on the previously empty throne. As his eye fell upon her she became unconscious, and could remember nothing more until she found herself on the beach at Raasay in the early morning.

The hours of this melancholy day wore slowly on, but no Eudæmon appeared. At last, towards evening, they forced open the door of his little turret chamber —it was empty. All his books and instruments were gone ; everything belonging to him or his mother had disappeared from the Castle. Even the harp itself, beside which so many pleasant evenings had been whiled away, was no longer there.

The only things left, and upon these Miranda flew with eagerness, were the chess-board, the wooden men he had so patiently carved for her, and the box to contain them. For long hours the poor child would sit as in a dream, arranging and re-arranging the motley pieces, softly laughing to herself the while ; for her mind was hopelessly gone.

Eudæmon had never wholly disclosed the fact that when they entered the enchanted precincts of Thuisto, any infringement of the rules prescribed must re-act upon himself. In his unselfish devotion, he imagined that if he alone fell a victim to the powerful sea-kings, his beloved and her mother would be saved. Freed at last from enchantment, he trusted that the Princess and her parents would then live on as happily as if no forfeit had been paid for Miranda's deliverance.

He fathomed not the unchanging love that had of late struggled into existence in the dreamy maiden's breast. In the terrible moment that by no fault of his own determined his fate, Eudæmon for once forgot his careful self-control, and clasped Miranda to his heart. In his dread father's presence he bade her a long farewell ; he knew not that the sorrow of parting would overwhelm her gentle spirit, and break her tender heart.

King Murdoch and his wife took their daughter by slow stages to her native country, hoping to benefit her by the change. But no following spring should ever re-kindle the roses in those waning cheeks—no mortal hand arrest the progress of decay. The faith-

S

ful Luachan could not be separated from her, he was her constant comfort and playmate.

There was a spot on the little Cumbræ where Miranda loved to sit and gaze across the Clyde's broad estuary to the blue hills of Arran. Perhaps their clear outline reminded her of the Cuchullins, as seen from Raasay. Perhaps being on an island, spoke to her of the halcyon past.

Be that as it may, one day, towards evening, alarmed by her long absence, the attendants sought and found her here, cold and motionless. One arm was clasped around Luachan's neck, the other, faithful in death, still pointed the golden needle to "the true and tender north."

They buried Miranda where she lay. On that far island you still may see the lonely tomb, beneath which the weary one is at rest, and drop, perchance, a tear over her untimely fate.

Yes! They are united at last never more to part! Behold, in the regions of eternal peace, a youth divinely fair, a maiden serenely beautiful. Together they bow before the Almighty Ruler they served on earth, and, as they cast their golden crowns at his feet, the tongue of the dumb sings sweetly, "God is Love!"

Castle Brochel was never more inhabited. Donald, a sincere mourner for his kind young master, could not bear to live by himself within its shadowy portals. He transferred what he needed to the shieling near at hand, and thence descending every day, kept all in readiness for the expected return of the youth he loved so well.

But the old man watched in vain. He was gathered at last to his fathers. The lonely, neglected Castle fell into decay, and still, through following ages, the well-remembered Enchanter returned not, to awaken with his light springing footsteps the echoes of that deserted abode. Desolation and solitude spread their wings around its time-honoured precincts, and cast a halo of their own over its crumbling walls.

Break gently, ye wavelets, on Raasay's lone shore,
Eudæmon shall roam on your mountains no more.
As fragrance distilled by the cold air of night,
So Absence and Time shall bring forth to the light,
The deeds and the virtues of one without guile,
Whose genius and wisdom shed light o'er your isle.
Mourn wildly, ye seabirds !—all nature make moan !
His chamber is empty—his footsteps are gone.
He toiled unrewarded—no guerdon he sought,
As soothing relief to the weary he brought ;
But the mother's soft tear, and the infant's glad cry,
The blessings of gratitude garnered on high,
Shall, e'en in his Home, 'mid the Regions of Light,
Add lustre untold to his coronal bright.

THE END.